The Divorce Group

A MURDER MYSTERY

Donna Underwood

abbott press

Abbott Press books may be ordered through booksellers or by contacting:

Abbott Press
1663 Liberty Drive
Bloomington, IN 47403
www.abbottpress.com
Phone: 1 (866) 697-5310

Because of the dynamic nature of the Internet, any web addresses or links contained in this book may have changed since publication and may no longer be valid. The views expressed in this work are solely those of the author and do not necessarily reflect the views of the publisher, and the publisher hereby disclaims any responsibility for them.

Any people depicted in stock imagery provided by Thinkstock are models, and such images are being used for illustrative purposes only. Certain stock imagery © Thinkstock.

ISBN: 978-1-4582-2004-2 (sc)
ISBN: 978-1-4582-2005-9 (hc)
ISBN: 978-1-4582-2006-6 (e)

Library of Congress Control Number: 2016902534

Print information available on the last page.

Abbott Press rev. date: 02/22/2016

A divorce group has just begun the first of eight sessions. The group of seven plus three facilitators meet at the Grief Clinic every Thursday evening at six p.m. for two hours. The clinic has experienced three homicides in less than two years and will soon be visited again by a stranger or someone closer to the participants with murderous intentions.

In appreciation to:
- Wayne, my husband who patiently read this book, made corrections and encouraged me to keep writing.
- Patty Clark for her many corrections and good suggestions.
- DeeAnna Galbraith, my editor. She did not give up hope that I would learn past and present tenses.

DEDICATED TO:

To our grandchildren:

Brandon, Jaime, Paris, & Quinn Houk

Xavier, Kira, Annaka, & Scarlett Reutzel

Bridgett, Carl, & Emory Underwood

Aliya & Jacob Topek

To our extended family:

Derreck and April Marshall and their children, Lauren, Vaughn, Hayden and Samuel

INTRODUCTION

The year is 2012 and Brooksie Everett is turning thirty. Miss Everett is the owner of a small office building located in downtown Whitefall, Washington, a town located about thirty minutes from Seattle. Thirty minutes on a good day, but on a bad day it can take an hour and a half to get to the big city. She rents space to three social workers and two psychologists. The social workers, including Miss Everett, also a social worker, take turns offering support groups for those grieving meaningful death losses or for those divorced or separated.

Brooksie Everett, Lucinda Chavez and, Rachael Young, are licensed social workers and have their own private practices and offices at the Grief Clinic, so named by Miss Everett for her professional building.

Last year was a terrifying and heart wrenching year for most everyone at the clinic. Three homicides took the lives of two previous clients and the sister of one of the psychologists, Dr. Sharon Primm. Dr. Primm was renting one of the offices from Miss Everett.

Two men who had been members of two different support groups, both widowers, were murdered by Dr. Primm's sister, Maureen.

Sharon Primm is serving a long sentence for killing her sister and now resides at Lancers Women's Prison. She was and still is loved and respected by the clinic's staff. They all considered Sharon's act a mercy killing, done to save others and out of love for her very disturbed sister.

This story is about the many motives and personal issues that lead some down the path of divorce, some to reconciliation, and a few who take more drastic measures such as murder. It begins with the interviews of perspective group members for the next scheduled divorce group.

CHAPTER ONE

I hung in too strong
And too wrong
For too long
Virginia E. Pipe, M.Ed.

The Interviews

Lucinda began, "I met with Melika first. She is thirty-two, married for twelve years and divorced two years. She is well-groomed, petite and in great shape. She has the most beautiful emerald green eyes that peek out from under long, dark eyelashes. Melika is well spoken and seems to understand the problems that are ongoing with her ex-husband. He keeps her involved with him by threatening to kill himself every time she tries to distance herself. I think she will benefit from the group. She needs help separating and prioritizing her personal needs from that of her ex-husband's. He manipulated her for most of their twelve-year marriage. Her ex-husband and her mother use similar behaviors to control their spouses.

"Next, I interviewed Shannon. She is forty-two, married for twenty-two years and divorced for three years. Her self-confidence was badly shaken by her ex-husband during their marriage and this continues to be a problem for her. Her only child, a son, is in the service. She is very proud of him. It seems that she is letting her past regrets get in the way of moving forward. I believe the group feedback will be beneficial.

"My last client was Jason. He is forty-five, married for close to three years and separated for three months, but still cohabitating. He was a middle-aged bachelor until he fell in love with a beautiful model. He said the first couple years of their life together were terrific. He went on to say in the last year she only seemed interested in spending much of her time with friends and shopping. When he placed a monetary limit on her spending, she changed completely. In the beginning of their marriage, Jason had cut himself off from the few friends he had so that he could spend every free moment with her. He is a CPA and employs ten others in his office. He can't understand what happened to their 'great affair.' Now he finds himself alone, and feeling 'lost in the desert'. He also mentioned deep concern for his wife because she seems depressed. He does not want to divorce her and hopes to learn enough to be able to win her back. He is articulate and I believe he will develop more insight while participating in group sessions. How did your interviews go, Brooksie?"

"I spoke with Cecelia, age thirty-five, married for four and one half years and divorced for eight months," answered Brooksie. "She is a practicing dentist, who describes herself as plain and overweight. Said she was swept off her feet by a good-looking man. During her second year of marriage, she pushed to have children. He deceived her by secretly having a vasectomy. It was only by accident that she discovered his surgery. Cecelia was good at describing her feelings. She sounded wise and has made an honest appraisal of her strengths and weaknesses. I believe she will be an excellent group member and gain useful information for herself.

"Ruth is fifty-five years old, married for thirty years and divorced for three years. She wore no makeup, and sported dull-colored, ill-fitting clothes. She could definitely benefit from a trip to the hair stylist, and a few lessons in applying makeup and wardrobe. She said her husband, George said he had had enough and was leaving. Which he did and divorced her soon after. According to Ruth he had been unfaithful one time and maybe more over the years, but she took him back. Said she ignored his supposed affairs because she didn't think she could raise the kids without him. She went on to say her religion teaches that divorce is a sin. She told me that her ex is getting remarried in two months to 'some young slut.'

"Their children have taken sides. My hope for Ruth is to understand how her own behaviors may have contributed to the family problems. I hate to admit this, but I have to fight my desire to prejudge this woman. I've never been married, and have no kids so I have zero experience with the challenges she has had to face. But she sure has a difficult personality. She talked nonstop and seldom listened. As a matter of fact, I found her to be as irritating as a fingernail running down a blackboard. This woman may be the one who teaches me some new facilitating skills. Perhaps group will help her accept and claim more responsibility for her part in the breakup.

"Gage was my next client. He is forty-eight, married for ten years and divorced for one and a half years. He had been married twice. He was eighteen when he married for the first time. The marriage lasted for one year and they have remained friends. He stayed single for twenty years and then met Gina. He was thirty-five and she was twenty-nine when they first met. They dated for three years, got pregnant and married. They have two children. Their son is ten years old and the daughter is eight. He told me his wife returned to school to get her degree when their daughter entered first grade.

"He's confused and sad about the divorce. They have joint custody of the children. Gage admitted having resentment toward his wife, for returning to school and eventually wanting to start her career. He said they must have grown apart because of the amount of time they spent separated."

"I believe the group will offer him an outlet for his feelings and he may gain some insight from the other members' remarks and experiences. He's interested in the well-being of his children and according to him, so is the wife.

"Kent was my last interview. He is thirty-nine, married for two years and separated for six months. He arrived at his appointment with a one or two day beard growth, eyes were red and swollen, with dark circles. He was expensively dressed, not that I know much about expensive wardrobes, but his clothes just screamed money. He is good-looking, tall, muscular, with a full head of dark brown hair and piercing blue eyes, the color of robin's eggs. I know the color well because I've had many robins build their nests in my trees and lay their beautifully-colored eggs.

"Just a side note, Lucinda. Kent talked about feeling devastated and confused by the separation. He spoke of his wife in very complimentary ways, but at the same time, I felt he was flirting in an almost subliminal way. His words didn't match his body language. I'm far from savvy on the "flirty" behavior of men, but I sensed some kind of tension. Not sure what it was. I would appreciate your feedback after you see him in group. You've had more experience with guys trying to get your attention than I have."

"I'll keep my eyes and ears open," answered Lucinda. "It's not that guys don't flirt with you, the problem is you don't recognize a come-on when it hits you smack in the face. Marino is a good example of your blindness. He was giving you 'that look' and I think you assumed he simply had an eye infection, a tic or some other malady. Brooksie, one of these days Rachael and I will take you out for a demonstration."

CHAPTER TWO

Anger is a condition in which the tongue works faster than the mind
Author unknown

Brooksie thought she would be the first to arrive at the office, only to find Melissa already at her desk and talking on the phone, which she hung up the phone as soon as she saw Brooksie.

"Good morning Brooksie. We're the early birds today. That was Shaun making sure I'd arrived okay at the office. He's a jewel. I'm not used to such thoughtful treatment. Maybe I've finally found the right guy for me. No more wandering eye."

"From what you've said, Shaun sounds like a keeper," responded Brooksie.

All of a sudden the front door flew open and a wild-eyed, unkempt man bolted in. He was waving his arms around, stared stupid-faced at the two ladies and yelled, "Where the hell is she? You tell Melika to get her butt out here now." He reached for something in his coat pocket and both women gasped.

"You need to lower your voice. Please take a seat and Melissa can get you a cup of coffee or some water. What is your name, sir?" asked Brooksie. Her heart had jumped into her throat and she barely recognized her own voice. She sounded much too calm.

Her legs were shaking. She hoped the irate intruder wouldn't notice.

"No. I didn't come here for a damn cup of coffee, I came to see my wife. I'm Willy Swanson."

Brooksie said, "Mr. Swanson, you need to leave immediately. We will call the police if you don't." She puffed up her chest trying to appear in charge and show a brave front.

"Go ahead, you home-wrecker. I don't give a damn what you do. Call the police. Maybe they will help me talk some sense into Melika."

Brooksie picked up the phone and dialed 911. She asked for immediate assistance to remove a very angry man who was making threats to the staff.

Mr. Swanson stood motionless. He was breathing hard. Tiny drops of perspiration were trickling down from his forehead to his cheeks and falling off of his chin. He made no effort to wipe his face. He appeared to be frozen in place. Time seemed to stand still, a few seconds felt like hours to Brooksie and Melissa.

"You tell Melika what happens next is her fault. She has only herself to blame. The kids will hate her forever. You tell her what I said." He turned slowly, almost in slow motion and walked outside, not closing the door. Brooksie and Melissa walked to the door. They watched him stumble back into a car, drop his keys, bend down to retrieve them, and then nearly lose his balance. By the time he opened his car door, a siren could be heard, and within seconds a patrol car pulled up next to his car.

"That's the intruder," screamed Brooksie to the two policemen. They exited their vehicle and began yelling at the man to get down on the ground and to put his hands behind his back. There was no visible resistance given, as Mr. Swanson knelt down and put his hands behind his back. He immediately started sobbing.

Everyone would turn to stare at her wherever we went. We have no children. We married six months after our first date. Actually, I asked her to marry me after eight weeks of dating. She turned me down and said we needed more time to get to know each other. I asked her again four months later and she accepted. I couldn't believe my luck. That was my happiest day ever."

Jason barely looked at anyone while he spoke, eyes cast downward. He was dressed in a well pressed, expensive looking suit, shoes polished to a high military style. Even though he looked as if he had recently visited the barber shop for a shave and haircut, his overall appearance was that of someone deeply troubled. His eyelids were puffy, his hands in constant motion and he sighed often. Gave the impression he couldn't get enough air with one intake.

"Half of the time I'm angry at her and at me, the other half of the time I'm down in the dumps. I don't understand what went wrong. I just want us back together again, the way we were."

A few of the members fidgeted in their seats, as if trying to get comfortable. Kent got up and went to the refreshment table, quickly followed by Gage. Both men helped themselves to coffee and returned to their seats.

Brooksie reassured everyone, "Sometimes it can be hard to hear these stories and you may feel uncomfortable. That's not unusual. It takes courage to share and it also can take courage to listen with an open heart and to leave your judgments outside this conference door."

"I'm Shannon, divorced three years and married for half of my life, twenty-two years. I have one grown son, Richard. He is twenty, and in the Coast Guard, stationed in San Diego. I wish he wasn't so far away. I have one very close friend and she has been very supportive. I don't know if I would have made it this far without her encouragement, but I can't keep leaning on her.

"I can't seem to motivate myself to move ahead. My ex-husband, Daniel has a girlfriend or actually he probably has had several girlfriends over the years. I'm lonely and scared. I feel like a nonperson."

Her voice cracked and Shannon dabbed at her eyes and blew into her handkerchief. She was quite tall, a big-boned woman. She was dressed in a dark grey suit, a white silk blouse and low heeled black shoes. No noticeable makeup and her hair drawn up in a tight bun pulled to the back.

There is a down-to-earth quality about her, someone you could count on in an emergency. Brooksie thought.

"I'm Cecelia. Married four-and-one-half years and divorced for eight months. My emotions go up and down like a roller coaster, dangerously close to going off the tracks. I thought I was the luckiest woman alive. Ramon was a dream come true for me. Boy, was I wrong. Now I'm embarrassed, and badly shaken by my tunnel vision. My ex didn't love me, he loved my money. I'm basically a very private person. This is difficult for me to talk about my personal life, not that I've had much of one to talk about. I don't even share my life with my co-workers or colleagues. I made such a fool of myself."

The room remained noiseless for a few moments until Lucinda broke the silence. "We know this is a difficult session, but if you will all continue to share, it will get easier.'"

"My name is Gage." He was wearing a short-sleeved collared shirt, Levis and tennis shoes. One gets the impression this was his go-to-town outfit. He looked freshly scrubbed, about 5'10" and his years in construction have given him a very toned, muscular body.

Gage continued, "Married for ten years and divorced one-and-a-half years. We have a ten-year old son and an eight-year-old daughter. My wife and I share custody. Gina and I love our kids.

this group can be helpful for those who are separated as well. Jason you and I are both hoping to save our marriages. I sincerely hope we are both successful. I desperately want to win back my lovely wife. So I would greatly appreciate any suggestions from anyone."

Kent focused on Cecelia. Cecelia looked away.

Glancing at her watch, Brooksie informed the group the time was over for today. "We ask you to do a short assignment and bring it to the second session. Here's your assignment: 1. Write three complaints your spouse has made about you. 2. Write three complaints you have about them. 3. Write the name of one of your heroes and briefly state why. See you next week. You can pick up a copy of this assignment on the refreshment table as you leave. We wish you all a meaningful week. See you next Thursday."

Tony, Lucinda, and Brooksie stayed behind after everyone left. It was their time to share observations and concerns about what took place in the session.

Debriefing:

Tony spoke first. "Since I am the new kid on the block, I don't want to step out of line, but Ruth's attitude really bothers me. I know my role is to be a quiet and respectful listener and observer, but is it okay for me to have my own personal opinions and simply keep them to myself?"

"What exactly bothered you about Ruth's attitude?" asked Brooksie.

"The way she was so degrading of her husband. It's hard for me to hear such blaming and putting-down. I'm working to hold back judgments, but Ruth is going to be one tough test."

"Ruth's remarks made the hair on the back of my neck stand up. I felt like jumping up and pounding on her," said Lucinda in a louder than usual voice. She continued, "I took a deep breath and reminded myself that Ruth was not my mother. This calmed me down a little. Tony we have our own feelings that need expression, and that is why we meet after each group session. We are just practicing what we preach or better said, what we teach.

"I noticed how you took a spring-like position in your seat. You reminded me of my cat when she gets ready to pounce on something."

"Was I that obvious?" asked Tony.

Brooksie added, "I also saw you sitting on the edge of your chair. You looked like you were holding your breath. I was afraid you had forgotten to breathe."

Tony laughed and said, "I'm going to have to work on keeping a more neutral look. I'll get better at it because I'm going to work hard on relaxed listening."

Brooksie shared her negative feelings about Ruth as well. "I felt angry and disgusted with Ruth. My heart went out to her long-suffering husband and their children. When my negative feelings start racing ahead I remind myself that this irritating person was once an innocent child and now has a story that needs to be told."

"Tony," Brooksie continued, "We all have our buttons. The solution or trick is to know what pushes our buttons, what the triggers are and then to work on a plan to diffuse them.

"Kent and Jason present different concerns, such as how to get a marriage back on track, rather than how to live with divorce. I believe this will be a learning experience for everyone in the group, including us. Perhaps those two guys will gain insight, when the others are sharing what they feel they did that was counterproductive to a healthy marriage.

"Since I've never been married, these divorce groups give me ample information that I hope may help me avoid common traps. Doesn't seem like 'They lived happily thereafter' is the ending of many relationships. I hate confrontation, especially the fighting kind. I want the affection part, the laughing, the sharing and the knowing I have a partner, but I'm not sure I could do a good job with lots of conflict. My mother was married four times and I never understood why she married the men she did and then I couldn't understand why she divorced them. Most of the people in my life have been on a human conveyor belt. The belt ran continuously in front of me. Those times it slowed down, I would start to feel a brief connection. Then, without warning, the belt sped up and gone was the relationship. The belt moved along again and another stranger would pop up. Eventually, I gave up on long term friendships. Now, I'm a little less gun shy, but I'm still cautious." "It can seem like a crap shoot sometimes. We all change and for different reasons," said Tony. "My wife's change came about because of mental illness and there was simply no way to know this in advance. We make decisions based on the information at hand and have to hope the changes are mostly for the good. I know a few married couples who say they love each other more as they get to know their partners more. I believe there are many successful marriages. I'd like to think I will eventually get a second chance."

CHAPTER FOUR

"He who knows others is learned.
He who knows himself is wise."
Lao-Tzu Tao-te Ching

Lucinda and Brooksie met at the Table Talk coffee shop for lunch. Rachael, the other social worker and others from the clinic considered this place their watering hole. Usually, two or more of them showed up every one or two weeks for a lunch break. Once in a great while Anita showed up. Anita had been a volunteer for other support groups in the past. At present she is a full time student at the University of Washington and spends most of her time with her studies. Anita was, and continues to be, a protegee of Dr. Sharon Primm, who remains incarcerated for the killing of her homicidal younger sister, Maureen. Anita is goal-directed and wants to be the best possible student in honor of Sharon, her mentor and substitute mother. She continues her special friendship with Sharon.

Dr. Primm killed her younger sister with a drug overdose to stop her from murdering another client of the Grief Clinic. Maureen was a very disturbed woman. She had had mental problems beginning in childhood after her mother died and her father forbade her and sister Sharon from any outward signs of grieving. Dr. Primm worked at the clinic over a year ago. Now she is a resident of the women's prison in another town.

Today, Lucinda and Brooksie are having lunch together. Brooksie asked, "Has your mother been leaving you alone this past month?"

Lucinda replied, "I changed my phone number and that really pissed her off. She could no longer leave nasty and guilt-sparking messages. So then she would come by my house and leave ugly notes, mainly employing guilt tactics. I didn't bother to read them after the first few that she stuffed in the screen door. About a month ago, she saw my car in the driveway. She banged on the door. I didn't answer. Needless to say, I haven't seen her since. Maybe she has finally gotten the message that I'm through being her whipping post.

"Brooksie quit rolling your eyes. I know you think I am being naïve, but I am beginning to feel stronger and better about myself. I'm not so willing to let mom or anyone, walk all over me. I've even talked to Tony about my mother. You know, he really is a good listener. I think he and I could become friends. Would you believe I've never had a male friend in my entire life? Actually, I've barely had any close friends. You've come to be about the best friend I've ever had."

Brooksie responded, "I'm glad and honored, that you consider me a friend. My childhood was much different from yours. For the most part I've been treated kindly. Even though I've had multiple step-dads; they've always treated me decently. Trusting people enough to become short-term friends is fairly easy for me. I think the toughest part was moving so often. Every year a new school, met new kids, and had new teachers plus the new step-dads. Friendships never lasted. Long-term relationships had no chance. Mom's multiple marriages and frequent changes of addresses didn't add to my sense of security or permanency."

Lucinda asked, "How is it going with Marino? He doesn't seem very easy to get to know. He's sexy as hell and apparently a damn good detective, but does he ever loosen up?"

Brooksie answered, "He seldom shares much about his personal life. He's intense, treats me great, is generous and affectionate, but sometimes he gets a faraway look in his eyes and I know he is light years away. There is definitely space between us. I'm more comfortable with a certain amount of distance. If things don't work out I've saved myself some grief. I've only had two boyfriends. Actually, I was engaged to my first boyfriend. We'd been together for almost three years when he was killed in a car accident. I hate to admit this, but I got mad at him for getting killed. Pretty screwed up, huh?

"Marino is only my second serious relationship. Abandonment is a dirty word in my world. I'm always expecting people to move away, move on, or die.

"We have taken a few long weekends together. As you said, he is sexy as hell, playful and I love being with him. A month or so ago we got on to the subject of kids and I said I would rather adopt because there are so many unwanted children who need good homes. Marino got all worked up and told me he would never raise someone else's kid. He wouldn't elaborate and said, 'The matter is closed.' Maybe this sounds strange, but I have no burning desire to be pregnant to have my own baby. This conversation with Marino has really bothered me."

Lucinda replied, "That's a given, the part about you and adoption. Just look at your adopted menagerie of dogs and cats."

"I have my dear Aunt Tilly and Uncle Joe to thank for those furry companions. Those two are so amazing. Saving animals is really my aunt's passion and Uncle Joe simply loves her and does whatever gives her pleasure. Although I believe he is a big-time animal advocate, just as she is. If I tell him an animal cruelty story, he tears up quicker than my aunt."

Brooksie thought to herself, *Maybe I'm just setting myself up to be abandoned again with the adoption issue. I get so torn up inside thinking about unwanted kids and pets.*

Lunch time was over too quickly and it was time to get back to the clinic. The issues of children and mothers would be some of the on-going subjects for another day.

There was a message from Marino waiting for Brooksie on her desk, Melissa, the clinic's secretary and in-house flirt, had written, "call Marino on his cell. If only he had a twin brother I'd be first in line."

Brooksie dialed his cell. He answered immediately.

"Hi Brooksie. Thanks for the quick call back. I just wanted to remind you about our dinner date at Richie's restaurant Saturday night."

"I'm looking forward to dining at your friends' restaurant.," said Brooksie.

"Great! How about an overnighter?" Marino asked.

"Feeling frisky are you?"

"I'm way past frisky, maniacal is more like it."

"I'll ask my neighbors to feed my pets in the morning so we won't have to get up too early. I like keeping you in the horizontal position for as long as I can."

Marino added, "horizontal is always great, maybe we could try something in the vertical position. Just a thought."

As she hung up the phone, she could hear him chuckling.

Melissa reminded Brooksie to pick up another message that had come in earlier. The message was from Anita. She wanted to make a date with Lucinda, Rachael, and her to go for a visit with Sharon on Sunday at the prison. Brooksie called Anita back, but no answer. She left a message that she would ask Lucinda and

Rachael if they could go. That is, if Rachael had returned from her vacation. Later that day, they both answered in the positive and all agreed to meet at the office and ride together. Brooksie thought to herself, *sometimes I think Sharon is doing more to be helpful in prison than we are outside of those confining walls.*

When Sharon was sentenced to prison, she made arrangements to help Anita financially. Sharon moved Anita into her mortgage-free home, paid her tuition and all other expenses so she would be able to complete the required courses, and eventually, fulfill her dream of obtaining her Doctorate degree in Psychology. Sharon had befriended Anita and her brother, Brad, long before the tragedy. Sharon treated and considered Anita a daughter, and her caring extended to Brad as well. They were Sharon's only 'family'.

CHAPTER FIVE

**Marriage does not begin or end
with paper work,
Nor does a divorce.**

Session Two

Kent arrived early looking more rested. He was casually and expensively dressed.

"Kent, you're almost twenty minutes early," said Lucinda.

"Guess I'm anxious to get started. I don't know what else I can do to get my marriage back to where it was just six months ago. My wife made me feel so special and important, like I counted. I loved pleasing her. It was so easy to make her smile and laugh. I finally felt I belonged. For the first time I felt needed and liked for just being me. I didn't have to prove anything anymore. I was finally in control of my own life; and what a powerful drug that was! I became addicted to happiness. Marlene holds the key to everything. Sorry, I'm just rambling, losing control of my mouth.

"Maybe I can help you with arranging the chairs or something else. By the way, that jacket you're wearing is flattering and shows off your great figure."

"Thank you," responded Lucinda. "It would be helpful if you would move the chairs in a semi- circle. Then if there is time left before group begins perhaps you would like to look over our selection of grief books for various losses. There are several that address separation and divorce issues."

Kent finished moving the chairs and wandered over to the bookcase. "I'm needing to get back together with my wife. Are there any books here with tips having to do with pleasing a woman or how to understand the fair sex?"

"On the bottom shelf there are books having to do with respect, kindness, honesty, and other attractive traits. Perhaps you would like to look those over," answered Lucinda.

Lucinda thought to herself, *He is sure one handsome guy, but I can't tell if he is flaunting his good looks or if he's not even aware of how he comes across. I wonder who or what he sees when he looks at himself in the mirror?*

Melika and Shannon entered the room chatting. They were soon followed by the rest of the members. Kent greeted both ladies and offered to get their coffee. Both women remarked on what a gentleman he was. Kent smiled, showing off his perfectly straight, white teeth, and dimples.

Gage and Ruth were busy in conversation while pouring themselves coffee.

"Ruth, you said two of your kids have taken their dad's side and you felt they've betrayed you. Why do you think they've done this?" asked Gage.

Ruth put her coffee cup down and standing straight as a Marine answered, "Because they've been lied to. They seldom go to church anymore and are running wild. Charity, my oldest, is nineteen. She does what she wants when she wants. She is dating a heathen and as far as I'm concerned, he is leading her down the road straight to hell.

"John is almost eighteen and he has always favored his dad. He told me I drove my husband away by always complaining. I admit, I have fussed a lot, but how else can you get someone to do what they're supposed to do?"

"Ruth, I made a similar mistake with Gina. I complained constantly about so many things and now I'm beginning to see how that helped drive her away."

Ruth roughly picked up her cup, spilling coffee onto the floor. "I married for life. I was following the church teachings of 'For better or for worse, till death do us part'! I did without many things I needed and wanted over many years, but I didn't break my vows. George never said anything nice about my cooking. He never complimented me about anything. You know Gage, after a while I quit caring and trying to please him."

Ruth bent over to wipe up her coffee spill, then walked over to one of the chairs and plopped down.

Lucinda welcomed everyone and began by asking each one to take a minute and write down some of the feelings they experienced over the past week. When they finished writing they could volunteer to read what they had written. *I would do myself a favor if I did the same exercise,* she thought to herself.

A few minutes passed and Jason said, "I don't mind starting off. I wrote embarrassment, bitterness, shame and emptiness."

Brooksie asked him if he would be comfortable elaborating.

"No problem. I am embarrassed to go to public places where my wife and I have gone. I feel like some people pity me or are thinking, 'I told you so.'

"I'm ashamed of my own shallowness. I picked a trophy wife, one who would make me look special. I married Loreli because she was physically beautiful. She made me happy day and night. She married me because she believed I had an unlimited money source. She saw an expensive car, fine home in a well-to-do neighborhood and assumed I was loaded. I believe I made her happy . I want the two of us to feel like we did in the beginning.

She always did things to please me and now she doesn't want to do anything with me. That includes intimacy. We don't go out together in public because she quit fixing herself up, at least around me. We both seem to be miserable. I go to the office every day, usually from 8 a.m. to 5 or 6 p.m., but lately I go earlier and stay later, no reason to go home. I know she goes to the gym most every day and has lunch often with others. I really don't know what else she does. We have a house cleaner so Loreli has few household jobs. We used to do fun things on the weekends, but no more. She just mopes around the house wearing bed clothes and looking out of sorts, even depressed when I'm home. She won't talk to me about what's going on. I'm getting worried about her and I can't seem to be of any help. Guess I don't feel bitter, just helpless and very much alone."

"How long have you felt alone?" asked Brooksie.

"Most of my life. That is until I married Loreli, at least for the first two years. In the last six months or so she wants to go out with her friends, not with me. That hurts. I swear I don't know what is going on. She is a mystery to me. Sometimes I think she is depressed, then bored and then she looks at me with a look I can't describe except to say it makes me uncomfortable. I hate to admit this, but I'm beginning to feel she never loved me. Only loved what material things I could provide.

"My parents lived separate lives. I can't remember any joint vacations. I usually went with my mother or stayed home with the nanny. I guess I didn't see how little they cared for each other. I'm not even sure if they even liked me or each other. I think my mother had many friends, mostly men. My father was preoccupied with making money." He lowered his head and his neck seemed to disappear under his starched collar.

Shannon said, "Your childhood sounds sad and lonely. Did you have any friends?"

"Not really. I wasn't popular. The only time I can remember any whisper of a social life was my last year of high school. I received a new Corvette for my seventeenth birthday. I dated a few girls, nothing memorable. I believe the Corvette was the attraction and not me." Jason swallowed hard and continued, "College wasn't much better. I was very serious, studied hard and that's about all I did. I guess I was never much fun to be around."

"Jason, have you or Loreli ever gone for marriage counseling or any type of therapy?" Tony asked.

"No. I've asked her to go and offered to go with her. She told me in no uncertain terms that there is nothing wrong with her. I was the one with the problems and being stingy was a big one.

"I have explained our finances to her and she seems to resent the fact we have to live within my means. I'm not what they call 'filthy rich,' but I am very comfortable. Loreli simply thinks there is no limit to my bank account. I had to put a stop to her credit card spending. She still has a credit card, but I put a reasonable limit on it."

"What does she say about you coming to the grief clinic every Thursday night? asked Tony.

"She doesn't know. I've told no one." Nobody said a word for a moment or two. At last Brooksie stated, "Jason, perhaps you would care to share your reasons for keeping your participation in this group a secret?"

Jason said, "Maybe in another session I will."

Melika chose to speak next, "I've written down sadness, fear and frustration. I don't understand why my ex lies to our daughters. He has said ugly, untrue things about me and to me, and in the next breath tells me how wonderful I am, and that he can't live without me.

"He calls me many times during the week and becomes very upset if I'm not there to answer his call. He calls me at home and at work. He accuses me of having a boyfriend, actually of having many. When I'm at work and lunch time rolls around I sometimes will go to lunch alone or with co-workers. He often calls me at work during the lunch hour and if I'm not there to speak to him, he leaves a nasty message.

"I've not dated anyone since our divorce. I'm not about to get involved with someone at least until the girls have finished school and go off to college. Wilson, my ex, is driving me to distraction. I'm afraid he will kill himself, because he keeps threatening to."

"Melika, you brought up in our interview that your mother had been manipulating your father for years with empty suicide threats," stated Lucinda. "What did your father do when your mother would make repeated threats against herself?"

"He would give in to her demands. He was a pro at avoiding any kind of confrontation. If he wanted to take a trip someplace and she didn't, she would throw a fit, accuse him of selfishness and not loving her. If they took any kind of a trip it was when and where she wanted to go and for how long.

"He was invited to join a men's bowling team and she started crying and said he just wanted to get away from her. Her tears were persistent and she eventually said, 'Go and have a good time with those girls at the alley'. Again he backed down and never mentioned bowling again.   "This sort of drama went on all the time while I was growing up. And look what I did. I married the same kind of person my mother was and still is. I have, to my shame, followed the same road as my father."

Lucinda enthusiastically spoke up, "You broke the mold Melika. You were strong enough to get a divorce. You are one gutsy woman. It takes courage to change old behaviors. A hero is someone who does something despite the fear. Time for you to acknowledge how truly strong you are."

Cecelia added, "I think you are brave and need to give yourself credit for being so courageous. You are not responsible for your ex-husbands life, he is. Your father set a very poor example for you to follow, but you are showing your daughters a healthier example. Good for you."

Melika bowed her head and began to cry softly. Shannon was seated next to her and offered Melika a tissue. She said, "You deserve much better. Actually I admire you. I wish I had half your moxy.

"Guess I'll read mine next." Shannon read, "Disappointment, hurt, disgust, and regret. I was married twenty-two years to Daniel. I was so crazy about him and I couldn't believe he wanted to marry me. Our wedding day was the happiest day of my life. I felt like Cinderella, my dream had come true. It quickly started to fade after the first six months of our married life. I gradually and painfully figured out I was the only partner in love with the other one. I stupidly and regretfully made up my mind to be the best wife I could be and then Daniel would love me like I loved him. It never happened. I regret staying longer than one year with a man who did not really care about me. This is also the reason for my shame and disgust with myself. How could I have had such little pride?

"Now, I wholeheartedly believe that self-respect and respect for all others needs to be taught from the first day of one's birth, followed by classes in school, beginning in the first grade through high school and in the colleges and universities.

"I alone am responsible for staying in such a demeaning and harmful relationship. I did do one thing right. I purposely taught my son that being valued is a birthright and to never forget that, no matter what.

"My son is my complete joy. He is loving, independent, has a healthy outlook on life, does a great deal of volunteer work and laughs easily and often. I failed in marriage, but I did okay in the parent department. He encouraged me to leave his dad behind many years ago. I felt somewhat like you Ruth, that marriage was forever, but I have changed my mind. When marriage becomes destructive it is more like death in slow motion, an unnecessary suicide. I don't believe that a loving God wants us to self-destruct."

"Your husband must have been blind to all of your attributes," offered Tony. "He had a woman who loved him and put her love into action daily, he was and is the loser. You made a life saving and loving choice."

"I agree with Tony," said Gage. "Shannon's ex-husband made a choice to be hateful and hurtful. Shannon, in my opinion, you made the right choice, even if it took you a long time. You still need to be proud of yourself. Twenty-two years is a long habit to break and you did just that. Congratulations.

"Now, for the next twenty to fifty years your life can be filled with peace and satisfaction. You don't have to place any limits or restrictions on yourself. What an exciting future lies ahead for you. Maybe you can start teaching self-respect classes. I'm getting carried away here, sorry."

Gage started to laugh deep from his belly and made a loud snorting sound. "I'm laughing because Gina would think I had just gone crazy and in need of immediate hospitalization if she heard what I just said to Shannon.

"Now onto the assignment.   I wrote down confused, resentful, lost, and regretful.

"Gina and I weren't kids when we married. We dated for three years prior, purposely got pregnant and joyfully married. We had a son and daughter and life was good. We were compatible in every way. We had purpose, we worked hard, played hard, raised two great kids, we both had an important role.

"Gina seemed happy. I know I was, but one day Gina announced she was going back to nursing school. In the beginning I encouraged her, but it soon became apparent that she barely had time to take care of the family. I was working long hours. Construction business was booming. Gina was either in school or studying at home.

"I felt like I was living with a roommate rather than a wife. We seldom argued, but the silence became deafening. Resentments began to build on both sides. Gina suggested counseling, but I refused, saying I was not the one who had turned our life upside down. I said I could hang on until she finished school and then things would get better. Then she said that she planned to go on and get her Master's degree and when finished, wanted to go to work and put her education to use.

"I blew up. Told her we didn't have a marriage anymore just an arrangement. She told me if I felt that way it would be better for us to go our separate ways. I asked her if there was someone else. She said absolutely not, that she loved me, but just needed more stimulation. She said that the children would be leaving home in the not too far future, and she was simply planning ahead. She added that she would be able to help us financially, especially if both children wanted to go to college. We argued, discussed, cried until dawn with no satisfactory resolution. We agreed to talk to a lawyer and the rest is history.

"Now I'm sorry I didn't go to counseling with her. Maybe a therapist could have helped me remove my blinders. Maybe Gina could have better understood my irrational fear of having a parallel marriage, like my folks had. Guess I will never know."

"I can certainly relate to your remark about blinders. It seems we both had parents who lived separate, parallel lives. Sounds like you had a good partner, but you simply drifted apart because of different goals and lack of communication. You were content to keep everything the same and she wanted to grow, to spread her wings," Jason replied.

"Gage, I can totally understand your wanting to keep everything copasetic," said Kent. "I too wrote down confused because I don't understand why I'm separated. I was ecstatically happy. I thought Marlene was happy also. We were well suited, sexually, emotionally, and socially. We both loved to dance, to have friends over, attend social events, and just to be alone holding hands and sitting on our porch. We could go down to the beach, spend all day talking and relaxing, just being together was enough. She loved buying me gifts, spoiling me, and I loved to give her long, sensual massages, which she dearly loved.

"My anger is directed at her sister. She tried, from the very beginning of our relationship, to keep us apart. Rayana did have some mental problems in the past, so I tried to be understanding of her condition, but I blame her for Marlene's distancing herself from me. Eventually Marlene would hardly talk to me. I tried to talk with her, but it was like she didn't want to be alone with me. She asked me to move out of our house, called it a 'separation,' but soon as I left, per her request, she wouldn't answer my phone calls."

"I don't give up so easily. I will find a way to help Marlene see how her sister has twisted and turned her away from me."

"What exactly did the sister say or do to convince your happy wife to separate from you?" asked Brooksie.

Kent went on, "I don't know what she told Marlene and I don't like speaking badly about my sister-in-law, but she did have a habit of gossiping, embellishing rumors she may or may not have heard. I would describe her as a drama queen, one deserving of an Oscar. Her own private life was boring so she would turn trivia into a full documentary. I also believe she's totally dependent financially on

Marlene's generosity. Rayana may see me as a threat to the lifestyle she has gotten use to. Marlene refuses Rayana nothing."

"Did you and Marlene ever go to a marriage counselor?"asked Tony.

"No," answered Kent. "Marlene refuses to talk to me about what is bothering her. She has refused to talk to me about anything. I feel like I'm fighting a ghost. Her sister has really done a number on me."

Cecelia stared, without blinking, into Kent's intense eyes and asked, "If your sister-in-law's only motive was jealously, I can definitely understand your anger. What is difficult for me to grasp is why your wife would so easily be swayed since you say you were both so happy."

"I agree with you Cecelia," responded Kent. "You would have to ask Marlene that question."

"Perhaps I will, if I get the chance," replied Cecelia. "Now to the assignment. The words that come to me are neediness, embarrassment, tunnel vision, hurt, desperation, loneliness, and lastly, lessons learned. Ramon was the first man to be so attentive to me. He was dashing, well versed on many subjects, could strike up a conversation with anyone and make all present comfortable. I felt desirable and appreciated as a woman when we were together. That was a first time experience for me.

"I dated very little up to the time I met Ramon. I'd been going to school full time, held a twenty-hour a week job and after finishing my education I went directly into a dental practice. I loved my career, was content with my life and then along came this handsome, Latin, eligible man who was pursuing me. Several of my friends advised me to 'take it slow,' and get to know this person. I chose to ignore their sage advice.

"I was deaf, dumb and blind to the advice from my old friends and to my own common sense. It can be frightening what a person will do if they want to believe the sincerity of the person pouring on the attention and flattery. All the compliments and adoring attention, although phony, can become like a drug addiction. Maybe there is even a touch of insanity at work. Delusional thinking that keeps reality at bay by the irrationalism of denial.

"I couldn't believe such a great looking, well-educated man wanted me. I didn't want to give our getting to know each other too much time because I was afraid the fantasy would disappear."

Kent was looking directly into Cecelia's eyes and said, "Perhaps your friends were jealous of your new found romance. It doesn't always take years to get to know how you feel about someone. I hope you don't give up on love."

"Kent, I agree there are those relationships that began with the myth of, 'The first time I saw you, I knew I loved you and I wanted to spend the rest of my life with you.' I don't believe all of those relationships that start with being swept off ones' feet always last. No, I won't give up on love, but I won't be wearing blinders or rose-colored glasses, if there is a next time."

Ruth was the last person to share, but it took some encouragement from the group. Ruth was wringing her hands and shuffling her feet. Her lips were pursed so tight that even air had to force itself through. Her back was ramrod straight and she appeared ready for a fight, like a boxer waiting for the bell to ring announcing the next round.

"The words I wrote down are the feelings I had last week. Betrayal, unfairness, deceit, lazy, immoral, wrath of God, justice, abuse, fear, waste and failure."

Brooksie asked Ruth, "Please say more about fear, waste and failure."

"My fear is what is going to happen to me? Waste is about all the years I was married, and failure is about church laws. Most of the feelings I mentioned actually started long ago. My dad was a doctor and my mom was a college professor. I was always overweight like dad but mom was thin, like a model. School work was hard for me. My daughter had to help me spell the words for this assignment." She paused and wiped her mouth and forehead. "All school work was hard for me. Some classes were simply impossible. I barely finished one year of college with C's and D's. So I decided to find a job I could handle. I worked as a waitress for a short time. My second job was driving a school bus. I was pretty good at that, but my parents were mortified. I was an embarrassment and a big disappointment to them. I had an older brother. He died in a car accident when he was twenty-one. He was a straight A student and was in his third year at the university. My parents never got over his death. I was fifteen when James died. I started going to church with Belinda, the only friend I had at that time, I found some comfort in her church. It was there, years later, that I met my husband-to-be.

"My parents are both very intelligent. I was such a misfit. My brother belonged in the family, I never did.

"It's a terrible feeling to think you don't fit in your own family. Talk about no self-respect. Maybe I could be the poster child for your class Shannon?"

"Maybe a before and after poster. You could be both the before and after," responded Shannon.

"That's a good idea," exclaimed Lucinda, with a warm smile.

Ruth continued, "To this day I have never received a birthday card or Christmas card that says, 'Our daughter' and the plain card is always signed, 'Your parents.'"

Silence hung heavy in the room for quite a spell. Finally, Tony broke the silence with, "I feel such sadness for the pain of your childhood and a strong anger at your parents for the way they have treated you. You did not deserve such treatment from anyone, especially your own parents."

"I agree that you have been unfairly treated," offered Gage. "I would like to have a few words with your parents and they would definitely not be words of praise."

Brooksie spoke up, "I want to thank you Ruth for your courage in sharing such painful memories. Since you have been able to say out-loud some of the real hurtful experiences in your growing up years you have made it easier for the rest to share their painful memories.

"Our time is about over for today. You all have Lucinda's, Tony's and my phone numbers. If you feel the need, please call us. Some sessions will bring up many kinds of issues that need to be talked out. Also, if you so choose, it is okay to exchange phone numbers. Group support can be very valuable."

Brooksie reminded the group of the assignment given out at the first session. "Since we are out of time, please bring the assignment from our first session next week. Lucinda, Tony and I don't feel it is necessary to be too rigid about what gets discussed. Members have a way of talking about what they need to share and air."

Debriefing:

After the members left the room, the three facilitators began to share their observations. Lucinda was first to speak up, "I don't quite understand the problems with Marlene and Kent. It doesn't make sense that she was so happy, according to Kent, and rather suddenly wants a separation, maybe a divorce."

"He seems like quite a woman's man," said Tony. "I see him acting the gentleman with the ladies. I'm not saying that it is wrong, just seems excessive. Maybe that is just me and my conservative, shy background."

"Well, I do get a sense that all is not what it seems with him, but maybe he just needs more time to settle down," offered Brooksie. "I believe he is trying hard to please all of us."

"Ruth's disclosure certainly gave me different feelings toward her. Her parents have brutalized their own daughter. Now I feel a tremendous compassion for Ruth. It 's so surprising to me to learn how a little knowledge about someone can turn negative feelings into more positive and kind responses," said Tony.

Brooksie and Lucinda both nodded.

"I get so angry and worked up when I hear about the cruelties that people do to each other, including the animals," added Brooksie.

They finished tidying the room, locked up and walked out to the parking lot. Tony waited for both women to get into their cars, start their engines and drive away.

CHAPTER SIX

Appearances often are deceiving.
Aesop *Fables*

The day after session two, a Mr. Chuck Edwards who identified himself as a private investigator called the clinic and asked Melissa if Kent Richardson was attending a group at the clinic. She told him she was not permitted to give out any information about anyone now attending a group or anyone who has ever attended a group. Mr. Edwards then asked to speak to the person in charge.

"Brooksie Everett would be that person. I will gladly give her your name and phone number. She will call you back as soon as she can. She is unavailable at the present time."

"I would much appreciate that. Thank you," responded Mr. Edwards.

After she caught up with some paper work, Brooksie noticed Melissa's note to call Mr. Edwards. While she dialed his number she felt her stomach tightening. She sensed Mr. Edwards was the messenger of some negative news. *I must be feeling the trauma of last year's tragedies. I've got to stop thinking negatively. The clinic is going along just fine.*

"Hello Mr. Edwards, this is Brooksie Everett returning your call." She began twisting several strands of hair, with her finger, an old habit.

"Thanks Ms. Everett. I need to know if a Mr. Kent Richardson is attending one of your groups at the clinic?"

"Mr. Edwards, everyone working at the clinic follows strict rules regarding confidentiality. I cannot say yes or no to your question."

"I do understand, but would it be possible for me to meet with you and tell you, not ask you, about Mr. Richardson?"

"Why do you think information regarding the person you named would be of any interest to the clinic?"

"I believe there could be a possible safety issue for my client or, at best, a well planned scam." "I will think about your request. Can I get back to you today by phone?"inquired Brooksie.

"I would greatly appreciate that, till later," answered Mr. Edwards.

Brooksie dialed the lawyer's office and left a message for Mr. Bench to return her call soon as possible.

Minutes later, she received a message from Melissa saying that Mr. Joel Bench was on line one. "Thanks for responding so quickly to my call. I've had a request from a Mr. Edwards, a private investigator, who wants to meet with me to talk about a client in my divorce group. I explained to him about confidentiality and he responded by saying he would not ask me anything about the person, but wants to give me information in case said person is attending one of our groups. If I make an appointment with Mr. Edwards, it would seem like I'm saying yes, the person you wish to talk about is in my group. So I need your expert advice."

"I take it that the person who Mr. Edwards is inquiring about is in a support group?" asked Mr. Bench.

"Yes, in a divorce group. He is separated and wants to get his marriage back on track. My gut tells me I need to hear what Mr. Edwards has to say." *I'd really like to stick my head in the sand, but that is what my mother always did. My stomach is acting again like a washing machine, churning up all the dirt and sending me to the bathroom.*

"The support group settings are far less private than individual sessions. The expectations of confidentiality in a group setting are less restrictive than with individual work. You should be on safe ground by simply meeting with Mr. Edwards and listening to what he has to say," responded Mr. Bench.

"My heartfelt thanks Mr. Bench for your assistance. I will meet the investigator and if I have further questions I will get back to you. Thank you again for keeping us within the law," responded Brooksie.

"By the way," she continued, "Lucinda, Rachael and I will need to make a joint appointment with you in the near future. We are working with Dr. Primm on offering workshops in a women's prison. We have many questions for you when we get closer to starting some of our joint workshops. Do you remember Sharon Primm?"

"Yes, Brooksie I do. What she did out of love for her sister and to save others would be a very hard thing to forget. By the was, how is she doing?"

"She is doing amazingly well. She's writing books and programs for incarcerated women to help give them hope and a future," said Brooksie.

"This new project you ladies are starting up sounds very interesting. When you get closer to offering your workshops I'll be glad to represent your interests and do my best to keep you out of hot water."

"Thanks again for your help Mr. Bench. Talk with you later. Bye for now."

The next thing Brooksie did was dial Mr. Edwards. He answered on the first ring. "This is Edwards."

"It's Brooksie Everett and yes I will make an appointment with you. How about today at five p.m. at the office?"

"Five p.m. today is great, but I would prefer to meet you some place other than your office. How about the Table Talk Cafe? It's only a few blocks away from your clinic."

"That will be fine. See you at 5:00. I'll be wearing a sweatshirt that says 'Best therapist is your pet. No judgments, great listener and cheaper'," answered Brooksie.

"Great sweatshirt. Do you have any pets?"

"Oh yes, and if you knew my Aunt Tilly, you too would have a house filled with furry therapists. At the moment, to the best of my knowledge, I have six dogs and five cats. That is, unless my aunt stopped by my house today, after I left for work. I'm extremely grateful my aunt isn't into saving bears, whales and gorillas."

After the phone call ended with Mr. Edwards, Melissa hesitantly walked into Brooksie's office.

"Do you have a minute," asked Melissa?

"For you, always," responded Brooksie. "What's up? You look a little peaked. Are you feeling okay?"

Melissa said, "Mr. Jason Woods stops at my desk every Thursday evening before his divorce group begins and shows me one or two pictures of his glamorous wife. He tells me how frantic he is to get the marriage back on track. He stated last Thursday he worries that she is becoming more and more depressed. What am I supposed to say to him?"

"What do you want to say to him?" answered Brooksie.

"I'm sorry about your problems. Maybe your lovely wife could also benefit from some type of group or counseling. Hopefully, you share your concerns with the people in your divorce group. I know many people have benefited from attending groups."

"Sounds like good advice to me. Melissa, Is something else bothering you about Jason?"

"Yes. The way he looks at her picture. Like he idolizes or worships her. He sort of creeps me out."

"Thanks for bringing this to my attention. Please don't ever hesitate if you have a gut feeling about anyone that makes you feel uncomfortable. Tell me or any one of the other staff members. Anything else on your mind?"

Melissa continued, "One more little observation. Kent is quite the flatterer. I can't tell if he is flirting or just likes to pay compliments. He certainly doesn't creep me out 'cause he is movie star gorgeous. Woman must fall all over themselves when he's around. I wonder if he is for real or just a phony. That's all. Thanks for listening, Brooksie. I'll get back to my desk, or should I say my observation post, ha."

A few minutes before five p.m. Brooksie heads to the Table Talk Cafe. Mr. Edwards was waiting for her at the door and says, "You were easy to recognize wearing that therapy sweatshirt."

They shake hands, walk inside and find a table toward a back corner of the cafe. Mr. Edwards is dressed in a pin-striped suit and shoes polished to a high shine. His salt and pepper colored hair neatly trimmed. Face is cleanly shaven. He appears to be in his early fifties. He has a professional appearance, but at the same time, a softness shining through his dark brown eyes.

Brooksie is dressed far more casually in her favorite sweatshirt and leather-strap sandals. Fridays she seldom makes appointments with clients so she dresses in a more relaxed manner. She keeps an extra blouse hanging in her office closet, in case a client stops by. Her hair was hanging loose, the sides pulled together in back by a striking turquoise comb. She carries a bright yellow umbrella, like she does most days.

Mr. Edwards said, "Love your sweatshirt Ms. Everett. My wife and sister-in-law would also love it. It would make great Christmas gifts for the two of them. Perhaps later you could tell me where to purchase something similar?"

"Bought the sweatshirt at Penneys and had the words put on at the sports shop." She began twisting her hair with her fingers, stopped abruptly when she became aware of her old 'anxiety relieving habit.' "What is it you wanted to tell me about Mr. Richardson? I'm not saying I know him from any group at the clinic. You do understand that?"

"Absolutely. I understand the importance of privacy and confidentiality. I have been hired by Ms. Rayana Jetson, Marlene's sister. Rayana hired me to gather background information on Mr. Richardson. She wanted a detailed account of his past and present activities. I have uncovered some rather disturbing facts about his past, which according to Rayana, Marlene had no knowledge of before their marriage. In fact, it seems he had lied about his marital history among other things. Up to now, I have discovered the he was married before using an alias, of Kent Rothchild. His wife's name was Raylene Whitfield, and she chose to keep Whitfield after she and Kent married. She supposedly died at age fifty from a heart attack. My investigative work showed that the doctor who performed the autopsy stated initially the cause of death was 'undetermined.' The doctor reported a large hematoma and bruise on her forehead above her right eye. She had been discovered by her husband at the bottom of the stairs. She had been dead approximately four hours before he discovered her and he said he immediately called both the police and the ambulance. His alibi checked out. The final report mentioned that Mrs. Whitfield had Scarlet Fever at the age of eight which weakened her heart, therefore, it became defective.

"Mr. Richardson was using the name of Kent Rothchild when he married Raylene. He was thirty-one when they married and thirty-five when she died. She was very well off, with no living relatives other than Kent. He was the sole inheritor. Shortly after her death, Kent Rothchild just simply vanished, no trace, nada. None of Raylene's friends had any idea of his whereabouts.

"I looked through old newspapers, in the library, and found a wedding picture of Kent, and Raylene Rothchild standing on the steps of St. Marks Church.

"I have the picture right here."

Mr. Edwards opened his briefcase and handed Brooksie the newspaper clipping, he'd had the wedding picture enlarged. There was no mistaking the man in the picture. Rothchild and Richardson were one and the same. The article was long and wordy about the bride, her expensive wedding gown and all her financial holdings. Very little was said about the groom. *Here goes my red flag warning, my stomach's becoming upset. Why can't my warning system be a dry throat or some simple tick. No. I always need a bathroom nearby.*

Next, Mr. Edwards began to fill Brooksie in on Marlene, Rayana and more about Kent.

"Marlene had been married once before to the CEO of a large and lucrative lumber company. At the time of their marriage, he was sixty and she was forty. She told me they were very happy for five years. He died in a plane crash. He was the pilot of his own plane. Three other employees were on board. All three perished. According to the newspaper article, they flew into a severe storm and crashed into a mountain. Marlene inherited a great deal of money and a fifty percent ownership of her deceased husband's company."

"She met Kent a few years later. A whirlwind romance followed and in less than five months they were married. She was forty-nine and he was thirty-seven. He was movie-star handsome and apparently knew how to woo the women. Much of this information was given to me by Rayana.

"Kent apparently told Marlene he was between jobs, but that he was a carpenter and had just finished building a house. He also said he did some bar tending a couple nights a week and worked in a real estate office most weekends as a realtor.

"That is how they met. Marlene was looking for a second home at the beach and Kent was the salesman.

"According to the sister, Kent manipulated his new wife into buying a second home on the waterfront for cash, and then put it in both of their names.

"I was surprised when Marlene interrupted her sister and said that was not true. She said that she was the one who insisted on buying the house and putting it into both of their names.

"Apparently, he was her trophy husband. He always looked great, could converse on most any subject and I guess made her feel like a queen for the first year or so. The sister said the arguments between Marlene and Kent began over his spending habits. Marlene disagreed and said that Kent didn't agree with her charitable spending habits. Stated she had no problem with his spending. Marlene did say, and I quote, 'I can't believe he would lie to me. He was always so attentive and treated me with such thoughtfulness and kindness.'

"Rayana said she was becoming afraid for Marlene's safety. Marlene practically whispered her disagreement of Rayana's statement, but only repeated how kind Kent was to her. Rayana loudly told her sister that she was always unbelievably gullible, and added that she had always looked out for her, but was never appreciated.

"At this point, Rayana stomped out of the room and Marlene made a hasty retreat chasing after her sister.

"I hope this information will be of some use to you. I don't really know just how you could use it, but I felt it could be important. I've done a lot of work with couples and domestic violence so I'm pretty sensitive to red flags. I feel an obligation to clients, or in this particular case, to the relative of a client to follow up when I feel a concern for someone's safety. Don't get me wrong, I'm not saying that Kent may prove a danger to Marlene, I think it is better to be informed than not."

"Mr. Edwards, I appreciate the sharing of this information and will keep it in mind," said Brooksie. "I've had little contact with private investigators. Your concern for safety issues is commendable. And rest assured all of us at the clinic always consider safety a priority.

"Please leave me a card if I need to get in touch with you. I do have one question. Did you find out anything about Kent's childhood and years before he married Marlene Whitfield?"

"No, I haven't looked any further into his past. Do you want me to?"

"No, I don't think it would be appropriate."

They shook hands, left the coffee shop and walked to their respective cars, as they waved their goodbyes.

Brooksie, thinking to herself *this divorce group is becoming more complicated every day. I'll soon need to share Melissa's and Mr. Edwards information with Lucinda and Tony. I'd better stock up with Maalox.*

CHAPTER SEVEN

Life is what's coming, not what was.
Dr. Robert Anthony - *Think Again*

As was her habit, Brooksie arrived early at the office. She wanted time to gather some books on grief for the trip to the prison. Sharon might find them useful. She had just chosen five books when she saw Anita's car pulling into the parking lot followed by Lucinda and Rachael. Brooksie watched the three women from the window, as they walked arm in arm toward the building. It gave her a warm feeling of friendship, like being surrounded by a heated blanket in a cold room, to see her friends together again. They had been bonded by the earlier tragedies and had remained close.

Anita was dressed in blue Levis, a white turtleneck and a canary yellow sweater jacket. She turned twenty-six this year and still had the sweet face of a young choir girl. Her naturally curly, long, dark chocolate hair softly framed her cherubic face.

Lucinda and Rachael both hugged Anita. Brooksie closed the office the minute she spotted Anita and gave her a bear hug. Everyone piled into Brooksie's comfortable Suburban, dog and cat hairs included, and off they went to visit Sharon at the prison. No one complained about the fur and numerous pet toys. They were all grateful to Brooksie for keeping Aunt Tilly away from their doorsteps. "I'm over the top excited to visit Sharon and to hear about the plans she has to share with us," said Anita. "Sharon told me over the phone she is secretly working on an idea for the inmates and we are included in her proposal. That is, if we agree."

Lucinda said, "Whatever she has been cooking up, will be worthwhile. The more I learn about her, the more I admire and respect her."

Lucinda and Brooksie both dressed in Levis, long sleeve colorful shirts and white tennis shoes. Brooksie's shirt is bright yellow to match her bright sunny personality. Lucinda is sporting a shiny black blouse which compliments her dark eyes and accentuates her honey blonde hair.

Rachael is wearing a silver grey pant-suit and a red turtleneck sweater which shows off her shiny black hair which she had pulled away from her face in a long ponytail. Her dark eyes are filled with life and anticipation. Rachael adds, "Sharon is truly brilliant. I can hardly wait to hear her proposal."

Brooksie put in her two cents, "I agree Sharon is a woman who can make things happen. I'm glad she included us in her plans. I feel honored to be invited."

The drive took over one and a half hours, but passed quickly with an abundance of laughing and meaningful conversations between friends. *Tragedies often act as cement that bond individuals together, sometimes for a lifetime,* thought Brooksie.

They spoke about how shocked they still felt that Sharon's sister became a serial killer.

"I don't know if I could do what Sharon did. Taking someone's life, but I do sincerely believe she made the best choice in a no win situation," remarked Brooksie. "I do fe I could kill in defense. I want to believe I would be brave enough to defend children, animals, myself, and others if there was a serious threat. Hope I wouldn't shame myself and act cowardly."

The other three passengers agree their respect for Sharon has grown tenfold. Anita added, "Sharon is more than a mentor to me, she is a mother, a sister, a friend, a teacher and most of all an inspiration. She is definitely the reason I'm working my ass off in school. I want to make her proud and to let her know her life is meaningful and valued."

The weather was cool and the trees were dense along the highway. Greenery was everywhere, many flowers beginning to open their beautiful buds as the sun's rays touched their dew-dipped petals.

"Here's the prison," announced Anita. "My heart speeds up every time I visit this place. I feel so sad that Sharon is living here. She doesn't belong here."

"No argument there," stated Rachael. "There are probably many women who don't belong locked up."

The visitor's car is directed through the gate and shown where to park. A tall male, noticeably muscled, gestured for the ladies to follow him. They entered through several huge metal doors and are led into an office. The sign on the door said Warden.

Dr. Florence James greeted each with a firm handshake. She wore a tag identifying herself as Dr. James, Warden. She told her guests to please sit down and explained a few of the do's and don'ts while visitors are inside her prison.

The group was escorted through several check points, and asked to leave purses and cell phones with a guard. Anita was permitted to carry in one notebook and a pencil. Soon they found themselves in a small room with five chairs and a table. Sharon sat quietly, hands in her lap, her eyes reflected a kind of calm. Perhaps she had found a sort of peace in this place. Long before she took her sister's life she had carried a heavy burden. Sharon had been her sister's keeper since they were children. The siblings had never been permitted to grieve openly after their mother's death. Their father remarried soon afterward. The stepmom quickly showed her true colors and became the wicked witch of the northwest.

Sharon stood up when her friends entered. She had always been such a classy dresser and her orange prison garb was in stark contrast to her friend's attire. Anita embraced her fiercely and Sharon tenderly placed her hands on Anita's shoulders, holding her at arm's length and gazed into her face.

"You look tired Anita. Are you getting enough sleep?

"I'm just fine. Are you okay?

"Absolutely. Obviously the fashion police leave a lot to be desired." Sharon chuckled.

Then, one at a time, each friend gave Sharon a hug, a smile and a peck on the cheek.

Right off, Sharon wanted news about the clinic and how each one was doing. Anita shared all about her classes and her 4.0 grade point average. Sharon beamed like a proud mother would at such good news about an offspring.

"It is so great to see all of you," beamed Sharon. "I would love to hear everything, every detail, but we have been given only a one hour visit. I need to tell you about my ideas and get some feedback.

"As Anita told you, I have written a book on the grief issues that many of the incarcerated women here share. I'm convinced that if this prison would offer a variety of support groups and/ or workshops for inmates, the recidivism rate would drop dramatically.

"I also believe the fights and open hostility would be greatly reduced. This place is a hot bed of past abuses, repressed anger and sadness. The lack of compassion for themselves or others, the lack of education, and the absence of hope, are all strangling the life out of many of these so-called criminals.

"There have been several murders here in the last two years. Rumors suggest that the perpetrator or perpetrators have never been identified or yet to be held responsible. I don't know if this is factual. I've been 'walking on egg shells' because I don't want to mess up any chance at offering workshops. Any questions are frowned upon.

"I've heard stories of unbelievable cruelties this population of women have experienced in their young lives. As you all know, the basis for a decent life are; kindness, respect, accountability, safety and a sense of being loved and belonging. Many of these women witnessed just the opposite: cruelty, fear, intimidation to name just a few.

"I'm not saying they were all raised in the same way or in similar environments. I certainly don't feel that as adults they can use their past to excuse their atrocious behaviors, but there is an underlying, silent grief. We know the past cannot be changed, but the feelings about the past can be. So, my idea is to initiate grief support groups, workshops and programs that teach some of the basic life skills. I welcome any ideas or suggestions from any of you."

"Your idea is fantastic. Have you discussed this with anyone here?" asked Brooksie. Her passion for stopping abuses of all forms of life, including man and animal alike, lighted up her face.

Sharon responded, "Yes, I approached the warden and nurse Maxine Stark with the subject. The warden is not the most pleasant person on the planet to talk to. She is very negative about most things. She curls her lips whenever I mention any kind of change to "her" prison. She did say she would think about some groups and programs. In her defense I add that she is overworked and understaffed.

"Nurse Stark got rather pissy when I talked about the obvious sadness and anger that is so prevalent on the wards. I think she has resented me ever since I arrived. She has been the day charge nurse for eons and I think she and the warden are buddies. The night charge nurses name is Mela Washington. She thinks we have a great idea and wants to help us."

"I love your plans," offered Rachael. "I've written grants in the past. Perhaps that would be a possibility to get some seed money.

"I'm getting excited about the whole idea of working with such a needy population. At least we wouldn't have to worry about getting clients to come to our offices. We would have a captured audience. I'd love to be one of the facilitators and whatever else I could do to help," said Lucinda.

"So would I," contributed Rachael.

Brooksie added, "Count me in. I can even visualize a program involved with training unwanted or abused pets for different purposes. Then the inmates could be the trainers. My Aunt Tilly would love the idea. What do you need for us to start doing immediately?

"Nothing for a while," answered Sharon. "Anita and I have been working on topics for sessions and other programs. We send stuff back and forth through the mail. Once we have a completed outline and lesson plans, Anita will make sure you all have copies as well as time to gather your opinions and input. We will then ask for another meeting. I'm hoping to be ready to present our proposal and outline for groups and workshops in a few months. Rachael, you have a good idea for trying to get grants to finance our classes. We can talk about this in more detail later."

"Our allotted time is almost over. My sincere appreciation for your visit, your friendship, and much needed encouragement. I can't begin to put into words how much this visit means. Thank you all."

Anita's and Brooksie's eyes began to fill with tears over flowing and much to everyone's surprise so did Sharon's. Soon all were weeping and hugging Sharon goodbye. The guard led the ladies out through the numerous locked doors. They walked like a group of mourners leaving the cemetery as they made their way to the car. A great deal of animated conversation filled the Suburban as they drove back to Whitefall.

All expressed their eagerness to volunteer time at the prison and to work with Sharon facilitating groups and teaching other types of workshops or classes. The consensus was it would be a labor of love and one hell of an adventure.

CHAPTER EIGHT

**Life has taught us that love does not consist
in gazing at each other, but in looking
outward together in the same direction.**
Antoine De Saint - Exuperym
Wind, Sand, and Stars

Saturday evening, Detective Marino and Brooksie went to dinner at Lucia's, a cozy Italian restaurant that is tucked away on a side street. Brooksie was wearing a light blue peasant blouse and a free flowing dark blue skirt that went down to her ankles. She knew this outfit was a favorite of Marino. Marino wore a white shirt, opened at the collar and dark blue slacks. The white shirt emphasized his olive complexion and strong facial features. He wasn't handsome in the usual way, but his presence was noticed by all the ladies.

"Sometimes Brooksie, you remind me of a young naive, vulnerable, and impressionable girl. Tonight you look more woman-like. Maybe it's the way your hair falls onto your shoulders or the outfit you're wearing. I almost wish we had forgone dinner and went straight to my house."

Brooksie smiled and touched his foot with hers under the table. She said, "We could skip dessert."

The couple was greeted by Angela. She owned the place with her husband Richie who was also a cop.

"Good to see the two of you again. It has been quite a while since you were last here. No?"

Marino answered, "Yes, it has been too long Angela. How's your ugly half?"

"Oh you know. Too much delicious food makes a man happy, but also fat. More to love so he tells me. What will be your pleasure tonight?"

"Whatever your specialty is, that's what we want. Okay with you hon?"

Brooksie responded, "Sounds great to me. Good to see you Angela. Some time I want to bring my co-workers here for one of your great meals."

"They will be most welcome. You let me know when and I make my most special dish," said Angela.

Angela brought a bottle of red wine along with two glasses to the table.

Marino listened intently while Brooksie told him about Sharon's ideas and how excited she was to be able to participate in the programs. He remained quiet throughout the meal, but when the pungent, sweet smelling rhubarb pie topped with vanilla ice-cream was served, he said, "I don't want to throw cold water on your enthusiasm, but I really don't like your friend's plan. The first problem I see is for your safety and that of your friends. You will all be placing yourself and the others in harm's way. The second problem I see is that you are going to feel sorry for those women who made bad choices and now are being held accountable. The third problem and most important one is that you will have less time for us and for you own practice."

Brooksie sat up straighter in her chair. She opened and closed her fists, trying to relax herself, inhaled deeply and said, "I'm really surprised at your reaction to the idea of helping women make better choices in the future." She could feel her face getting hot and her hands beginning to tremble. "I've seen firsthand, just as you have, the devastating results of grief not given its time and place. You know as well as I do that the wounds of the past can reopen and become dangerous motivators of destructive behaviors. The jails are filled with festering humanity.

"How can you so easily forget Sharon and her crazed sister. You saw for yourself that a fine woman could kill her own beloved sister. It was a very compassionate and courageous act in my opinion." Her voice had gone up an octave and she took a few deep breaths trying to appear calm.

"Both of those women were driven by insensitive and cruel adults. The death of their mother when they were both young started a downhill landslide pushed by their ice-cold father and mean witch of a stepmom.

"Sharon is working hard, living in a damn prison, yet trying to empower others. Hoping to help them make their lives better. Her own future is bleak, but she's making every effort to bring about a positive difference for others, despite her own horrible future. I am going to do whatever I can to be a part of her plan, if she gets permission for her programs and for outside help."

Brooksie downed her glass of wine and poured herself another one. Her lips were pressed tightly together and her chest moved noticeably taking in deep breaths.

Marino answered in a lowered tone, "Let's not argue about something that hasn't happened yet or maybe never will. I would be very surprised if any prison, for men or women, was to allow non-employees to work inside with the inmates on a regular basis.

"You are also forgetting that your band of helpers would be putting other law enforcement employees in danger. They would have to be watching out for your group's safety plus keep everyone else safe.

"There are some women incarcerated who I wouldn't want to meet in an alley. They can be as dangerous as men. They are simply more clever, better actors, and more devious.

"You are far from street wise and much too trusting. A sociopath would have a heyday with you."

"I've not been around many criminals that's true," said Brooksie. "But I've had my experiences with many damaged or better said, injured adults. Many of these wounded souls have had difficult beginnings. Our childhoods don't necessarily condemn us, but they do shape our attitudes.

"Caring parents are expected to furnish tools for navigating the obstacles of life and to model constructive ways of living. I doubt many of the people you come in contact with had anything close to great role models."

"Damn it Brooksie, you always want to excuse the shitty behavior of the scum bags. You always make the parents the bad guys. It's the guy who commits the crime who is the responsible one, not his screwed up mother or fucked up dad. You've got your head in the sand."

Brooksie picked up the empty bottle of wine and looked for Angela. Not seeing her she stared at her companion, trying to slow down her breathing and stop her hands from shaking. "We see the world differently. I like my view better than yours."

Marino answered, "Let's not talk about this anymore. We just had a great meal so let's not spoil the rest of the evening. How about we go on home. Your menagerie has given you permission for an overnight at my house and we are wasting precious time."

"Blake, we have very different ideas about some issues very important to me. Maybe you're right. This isn't the best place or time to work them out.

"You've dampened my spirit. You're going to have to work hard to make up for throwing cold water on my enthusiasm on my new projects. Any ideas?" asked Brooksie.

Marino smiled his dimpled, sexy smile and said, "I can start by warming you up in a hot shower, then we will see just how dampened your spirit really feels."

Thinking to herself, *I really want to go home and surround myself with my precious pets. I'm ignoring the red flags and I know it. I'm such a coward and a hypocrite.*

Marino paid the bill, they said their good-byes to Angela and drove to the detectives house. Not much was said on their ride to his house. Silence can sometimes be deafening.

CHAPTER NINE

Cruelty is fed, not weakened by tears.
Publelius Syrus
Maxims

Session Three

The group members chatted amongst themselves, leisurely picked a seat and sat down. Tony and Lucinda choose chairs opposite each other and Brooksie sat down in the only unoccupied chair remaining.

"Good evening everyone," said Brooksie smiling at each one. "We will begin this session with the assignment unless someone needs to share something about the previous week."

Jason spoke up, "I'm not sure what this means, but Loreli's actions or I should say non-actions are worrying me. I decided to tell her I was enrolled in a support group. She said she was surprised. but glad I was doing something.

"She still isn't bothering to put on makeup and mopes around the house when I'm home from work. She seems to be totally disinterested in how she looks. This is a big change for her. She was very clothes-conscious and always fixed her face and hair first thing in the morning."

Lucinda asked, "Has your wife had episodes of depression in the past?"

"I'm not sure. I do know she has some pills that she takes with her coffee every a.m. I've never asked her about them. I thought it was a woman thing and I didn't need to know," answered Jason.

How do you feel about simply asking her if she is having a problem and how you can help?" responded Lucinda.

Jason replied, "I can give it a try. Thanks for your suggestion. Now, I'm willing to get on with our assignment. Number one, Loreli would say I'm cold, stingy, and controlling. Number two, I wrote, she is greedy, narcissistic, spoiled and distant. Number three is John Wayne because he was a take charge sort of man and everybody listened when he barked out his orders or wishes. I also picked a mix of James Bond and General Patton."

Brooksie asked Jason, "What do you think your wife is doing on the nights you come to group?"

"I imagine she is sitting in front of the TV, dressed in her bathrobe and drinking tea or sipping wine."

"Do the two of you go to church?" asked Ruth.

"No we don't. Do you think that would help?"

"Well it sure as heck wouldn't hurt or make anything worse," responded Ruth.

"I'll run that suggestion by her if only to see her reaction. Thanks for your concern."

"I don't know what George would say for the number one question," responded Ruth. "Probably I was too pushy, too focused on the children and went to church too often. He told me a few times that I was too demanding, critical and talked too much. Number two, I wrote, he lacked ambition, unfaithful, too quiet, lacked appreciation, and paid no attention to my needs. I had trouble picking only one hero so I picked two. First one is Mary, mother of Jesus, because everyone looked up to her as a saint. My second one is Hiliary Clinton because she is a lawyer and very smart. I have always dreamed of being smart, to be good in school and bring home all A's on my report card. I bet Mrs. Clinton was an A student."

"I don't mind reading mine next," said Gage. Gina would say I'm too unreasonable, selfish, ignores her needs, boring, and stubborn. My number two; I feel like she lost interest in us, selfish, stubborn, ignores my needs and too career motivated. One of my heroes would be Abraham Lincoln. He was wise, kind, fair, courageous, and wasn't afraid to do what he believed was right. He was an educated man who had all the right words and made speeches that we still quote today."

"I also admire Lincoln, Gage. He wasn't a handsome man according to the majority of society standards, but he was a man of substance," added Cecelia. "I wrote Ramon was dishonest, lacked integrity, cruel, two-faced, a leech, and shallow. I think he would say I'm too suspicious, naïve at times, too smart, too trusting, too plain, and boring. One hero would be the movie star, Sandra Bullock because she did not put up with infidelity. My all time hero is Helen Keller for her unbelievable determination to live, thrive and teach despite her many difficult challenges."

"I really liked this assignment," said Melika. "Made me think about what truly matters to me. I believe my ex would say I'm selfish, thoughtless, neglectful, mean, a terrible wife, and I always put him last. I wrote about him that he is suffocating, self-serving, needy, hateful, a liar, immature, manipulative and sneaky. My hero is Michele Obama because she is an attorney, wife and mother and seems to be doing a good job with all three roles."

Kent said, "Marlene would say I'm too affectionate, too social, and opinionated. I see her as gullible, too generous, and too loyal to her sister. The hero I chose is Robin Hood. He is the all time good guy, loved by all except the greedy ones. Plus, I've always wanted to be as good as the American Indians riding horses. They make it look so easy in the movies."

"Guess it is my turn," said Shannon. "My ex would say about me that I'm unattractive, stupid, wimpy and complain too much. My words for him are; mean, womanizer, likes to degrade, liar, unfaithful, and vain. The hero I picked surprised me. Elizabeth Taylor has been married many times, but she was always generous, interesting, brave, beautiful, loved her family and fought for a cure for AIDS."

Brooksie asked, "Were any of you, besides Shannon, surprised by what you wrote?"

"No, not really,' answered Jason. "Loreli wanted me to be more affectionate in public. She would ask me to hold hands, slow dance up real close and kiss anytime even in public places. That's just not me. First two years of our marriage I spent tons of money on her clothes, jewelry, furniture, trips and so forth. When I stopped going overboard with letting her buy whatever she wanted she called me stingy and controlling.

"So I began to see her in a different light. She was no longer interested in pleasing me. I had become an ATM and nothing else. She started to remind me of my mother, not a great memory. Lately my feelings have turned around and I want us to be like we were in the beginning, with both of us trying to make the other happy. I'm going to do whatever it takes to get us back on track.

Kent said, "Jason, you and I are very different from each other, but at the same time we do have some commonalities. In my case, my wife is the ATM. She is also the one who is extremely generous. She buys and buys mostly for others, including me, especially for me. I could pack up in two suitcases what I owned when we first married. Now I have the wardrobe of a king. So I'm not at all surprised what I wrote down about her being too generous.

"I need to add, there was a time before when I was doing quite well financially. I made some poor choices and I have learned from my mistakes."

Tony asked, "Can you be a little more specific as to why you think she is gullible and too loyal?"

"I will try," answered Kent. "I believe her sister is jealous of our relationship. She has had many boyfriends, but nothing ever lasts. Eventually the guys dump her. She is critical and picky. I think she drives them away with her demands and greediness. She wants her sister all to herself, her time, her attention, her thoughts and her money. I am aware the two sisters have been very close most all of their lives and our marriage has upset Rayana's plans. Maureen does not see how manipulative her sister is. Also Maureen is what some would call an easy mark. She can be talked into giving money to almost any and every cause. She has been taken in by several scams in her life. Maureen says I'm too suspicious when it comes to fund raising.

"I admit I have not been a good steward of money in the past, but I've learned caution is a good thing.

"Jason, I can relate to what you said about feeling uncomfortable with public displays of affection. Maureen also complains of that. She has told me I embarrass her with my 'playfulness.'

"This is one behavior I'm certainly willing to change, at least to lessen. Hope I've been more specific Tony."

Tony responds with an affirmative nod.

When Shannon's turn came up she shared, "I was surprised how easy it was to describe Daniel in such an unflattering way to actually put on paper what an anchor he truly is. Why do I continue to put myself and my wonderful son through his crappy behavior. I let myself and my son down by tolerating Daniel's cruel and self-serving ways. I feel like I've acted too late. I have hurt my son for many years because I didn't stand up for us. So many regrets and no way to undo the past mistakes."

Kent added, "Never too late to change our reactions and behaviors, Shannon. Have you shared your feelings with your son?"

"No. I'd be too ashamed and embarrassed to admit what a coward I've been."

Lucinda spoke, "You have told us how proud you are of your son and his career choice the Coast Guard. It might surprise you what your son thinks of you. You said earlier you son had encouraged you for a long time to leave his dad. Perhaps the next time you visit him you might ask him how he feels about the divorce and the fact that you initiated it."

Melika offered, "Shannon you and I are kind of in the same boat. We both let our partners dominate us. It is like we gave away our oars and let them do the rowing. We didn't stop them and demand a change of direction. Now we both have a chance to be captain of our own boats."

Lucinda, with noticeable animation of hands and her volume turned up said, "Wow! What a great analogy. I can definitely relate to both of your situations because I allowed my mother the same control. I will admit it has been tough making changes, but definitely worth the painful effort. I've had to bite my tongue, shed a few tears, shout out many profanities in the safety of my shower, of course, even fantasize her demise in many unpleasant ways. That's truly embarrassing to admit, but at the same time those terrible thoughts are a call for action; constructive action on my part. Most importantly, understanding and accepting the fact my mother will probably never change so I must let go of that hope."

"I've never had to deal with overpowering parents, quite the opposite, more like absentee parents. My need was and continues to be more about letting go of how I wanted my mother to be and simply accept what was and continues to be", stated Brooksie.

Cecilia began, "I'm surprised I wrote the word cruel. Cruel acts are deliberate. They are meant to cause pain. My choosing the word cruel for Ramon helps me to see us both in a different light. Ramon the predator, and me the prey. The prey are vulnerable, and clever. They are clever because they often outsmart the stalker. I'm glad I'm not like Ramon, a predator and a man without integrity, honor or compassion."

Gage followed with, "I agree with you Cecilia that much of the shit taking place in this world of ours is caused by the stalkers. Those people motivated by greed, lust, hate and fear.

"I'm not surprised by what I wrote, but I'm very surprised how the words unreasonable, selfish and boring make me feel. It was like a slap in the face and it hurts. I have been treating my wife in an unreasonable and selfish way. Maybe I've been expecting her to understand more than I have a right to. Why should she have to make up for my parents' behaviors? I have been on a "me me" campaign for a long time. Life is boring with a person who refuses to make changes. My wife's world was shrinking and turning colorless. I know it takes two to tango, but I wasn't even willing to try any of the dance steps. I didn't even move my feet. Where do I go from here?"

"Would it be possible for you to call Gina and make a date, some place away from your children?" asked Tony? "Then you could say to her what you have just said in this group. All you would have to do is listen to what she has to say."

"That's a great idea, Tony. Yes I will call her, but I'm already nervous. What if she refuses, then what?"

"Then you will need to figure what your next step will be," offered Brooksie.

Ruth squirms in her chair and tapping her fingers on her purse, like someone playing an invisible piano. "My answer is no. Everything I wrote down is how I see it. I have lived up to my vows and he has not."

Tony responded, "I wonder how your ex felt when you called him a loser? Also how do you think your children feel when you call their dad a loser?

Ruth answered in a shrill voice, "How do you think I feel about never having the things my parents and neighbors have? How would you feel if you had to shop for secondhand clothes for yourself and kids?"

"You didn't answer my questions, Ruth."

Ruth responded, "It was the truth. What was I suppose to say to their dad? Was I suppose to lie and say, 'You are such a great provider? Everyone in the neighborhood envies us.' I don't lie."

"I'm going to repeat the question to you because this support group is about feelings," added Brooksie. Feelings need identifying, acknowledging, owning them and hopefully learning compassion for oneself and others. Ruth how do you think your ex felt about being labeled a loser? What feelings do you believe your children have about your name calling of their father?"

Ruth responded, "I suppose I made him feel bad. I know two of my children don't like how I talk about their father. I think they are angry at me and embarrassed for their dad."

"Thank you for putting a feeling and the word loser together," said Tony.

Shannon joined in, "The word loser pushes a button for me. A loser denotes worthlessness, and lack of potential."

Brooksie suggested the members give her words that come to mind when thinking about a loser. "I will write them on the blackboard."

All of the members, except Ruth, voice a word or two and Brooksie wrote it on the board. The words that she wrote on the blackboard were: something missing, not good enough, hopeless, damaged, inferior, unwanted, in the way, and disposable.

A few minutes pass and Ruth said in a muted voice, "I never thought one little word could be so hurtful."

Lucinda addressed Melika. "Would you like to share what you have written?"

"I'm surprised just how baby-like, so narcissistic I think Wilson is. I made myself deny just how hopeless our situation truly had become. I don't believe he will ever grow up and realize he is not the center of the universe. I'm not going to let him be such a distraction in my life anymore. I always want to fix things, make everybody happy. I guess that sounds pretty arrogant and foolish. I must admit I do feel like a failure as a wife and that hurts."

Kent added, "I also feel like a failure. I've depended on my style, manners, looks, and social skills, but down deep I've never had much confidence in my character. I've given my best to Marlene and it obviously hasn't been enough. I definitely feel like a loser. I can relate to every one of those words written on the blackboard. What confuses me the most is up till a few months ago my wife seemed very content and in love. I just can't figure out what changed her."

"Perhaps you could send her a note or call her and invite her to a public place for a talk," offered Lucinda. "Maybe she would be willing to meet you at her accountant's or lawyer's office. Just a suggestion, Kent.

"Our time is up for today. This has been a fruitful and meaningful session. Remember you can call us if you have questions or concerns.

Debriefing

"Tony, you did a good job of gently leading Ruth to some needed insights," replied Lucinda.

"Thanks. I felt like I was walking on some very thin ice. Brooksie, you helped me stay out of deep water. It is a mystery to me why Marlene is not talking to Kent. I wonder if he had some problems in the past that are coming back to bite him in the behind?"

Brooksie said, "I talked with a Mr. Edwards a week ago. He is a private detective and asked questions about Kent. I only listened to what he had to say because of confidentiality issues. So I didn't say that Kent was in one of our groups. He gave me some rather disturbing background information about Kent. He showed me a picture. It was a wedding picture with another woman many years ago. He used a different last name. He was calling himself Kent Rothchild then. The lady was about ten years older than Kent and was a wealthy widow. Kent was thirty years old and the first wife was forty years old. Apparently, her first husband died in a plane crash. It seems he left her very well off. Kent was working part time as a real estate agent and that is how they met. Carolyn Whitfield was looking to buy a second home on the beach. He sold her a home and they married a few months or so after their first date. Approximately five years later, she died of a heart attack. Kent supposedly inherited a vast sum of money. According to Marlene's sister, Kent never told Marlene about his previous marriage. Kent was apparently using an alias when he married his first wife.

I spoke with the clinic's attorney, Mr. Bench, and asked him if we should inform Kent of the private investigator and his report. He suggested we wait for a few more sessions to be completed. He thought there could be a possibility Kent would talk about his past in the group and that would be best."

Both Tony and Lucinda are staring at Brooksie, speechless.

"Why didn't you mention this before today?" asked Lucinda.

"What are we suppose to do now?" Lucinda and Tony said in unison.

Brooksie hesitated before answering. "I was hoping Kent would clear up some things without our needing to say anything and I wanted to check with Detective Marino to make sure the private investigator was on the up and up. I will ask Marino to do whatever background check he can in the next day or two.

"I think we should pay close attention to Kent's words and moods. We don't know how much Kent's wife knows about his past. He may have told her everything about himself long ago. We just don't know. If he hasn't been upfront with her, then he may have a valid reason for withholding such information.

"I think we need to remain focused on the group as a whole and simply be watchful and attentive to details.

"I want the three of us to be on the same page and to decide if we want to invite Kent, his wife and the private investigator to meet with us. Do we share the report or do we first inform Kent about the private investigator and the report? Let him make the decision about informing his wife of the report.

"I have my preference, but I want to know what you both think would be the best action to take."

"I, for one, think we should tell Kent privately about the report and listen to what he has to say," answered Tony.

"I'm in complete agreement with Tony," said Lucinda.

"I agree with you both. I will call him and ask if he wants to meet with us and Mr. Edwards. I will simply tell him we have become aware of some of his personal background information and would like to hear his response. How does that sound?"

Both Tony and Lucinda nod in the affirmative.

"Now, I believe we need to remain focused on the group as a whole and simply be watchful and attentive to details. I am going to discreetly pay attention to Kent. Hopefully without acting like a spy in a slap-stick kind of comedy.

"I would like to say that I appreciate the participation of the members and the blackboard work. I've never thought about using a board as a tool before today, but I will from now."

Lucinda said, "Before we go our separate ways, I want to tell you, Brooksie, that my mother left me a phone message asking me to come to dinner at her house this coming Wednesday. I don't trust her motives and do not want to see or give her another chance to be a witch. I don't know what the right thing to do is."

"Lucinda, I know you are asking Brooksie, but I do have a suggestion," inserted Tony. "How about saying you will only go if you can bring a friend? I'll be glad to accompany you; that is if I qualify as a friend. If she is truly throwing out the olive branch then she will be gracious. If not, then she won't be able to hide her hostility."

"What a kind and interesting offer, Tony." answered Lucinda. "I'm going to take you up on it. Yes, I definitely consider you a friend by the way. Are you free this Wednesday evening?"

"Yes I am. If your mother is agreeable to my company. Can I pick you up or do you want me to meet you there?" asked Tony.

"I'll call mom tonight. Then I'll call you right after that and we can make plans for who drives."

"Sounds like you two have come up with a fine solution. Let me know how it turns out," said Brooksie.

Brooksie stopped on her way home after the evening divorce group and did some animal food shopping. After the noisy, and wet nose greetings from her pet companions she picked up her phone messages. There were two messages. The first one was from Aunt Tilly reminding her of Sunday dinner. The second one was from Melissa. She said she was at The Barn with her boyfriend Shaun and she saw someone she didn't think she was suppose to see out and about. "I'm concerned and puzzled by the presence and actions of this person. Could you please meet me tomorrow morning at the office about seven thirty? Sorry to bother you, but I think this may be important."

Brooksie decided it was too late to call Melissa back. She'd see her tomorrow morning.

CHAPTER TEN

**They who go feel not the pain of parting;
it is they who stay behind that suffer.**
Henry Wadsworth Longfellow
Michael Angelo

Friday morning Brooksie arrived early at the office in order to meet Melissa as planned. Melissa's phone message sounded strange and it piqued Brooksie's curiosity. Brooksie busied herself making coffee and clearing the junk mail from her computer.

Melissa was a no show by 8:00 a.m., Brooksie began to feel anxious. She kept glancing at her watch.

"Good morning Brooksie. What a fine day it is," said Lucinda, who cheerfully walked into her co-worker's office.

Brooksie responded, "Yes a wonderful day and I hope it continues to be beautiful. I was supposed to meet Melissa here at 7:30 this morning, but she hasn't shown up and I'm becoming concerned. She left me a message last night around seven o'clock or so saying she needed to tell me something important. She was at The Barn with her new friend Shaun. She saw someone there who really surprised her. She added, I would be interested in the identity of that said person. She asked me to meet her this morning. I'm going to call her."

After two attempts at calling Melissa's number with no answer, Brooksie asked Lucinda if she would drive over to Melissa's house with her.

"Absolutely, maybe she's sick or maybe she simply overslept. Wait, I just remembered I have a client this morning."

Tony quietly arrived and overheard the conversation. He asked, "Has she ever done this before, not show up or not call in?"

"Never," responded Brooksie. "She has always been 100% dependable. She's never let her night life interfere with her day job. I'm going to call Marino and ask him to meet us at her house. I don't want to embarrass her, but I have a bad feeling about her absence. I'm fighting my urge to think about worst-case scenarios." She closed her eyes in an attempt to stay calm.

Brooksie placed a call to Marino at the police station. Luckily, he was already at his desk. Her voice quivered, she tried unsuccessfully to sound calm and in charge of herself. She gave him a short summary and Melissa's address. They agreed to meet there in half an hour.

"Tony can you wait here for Rachael or Don and ask one of them to cover the phone?"

"I'll be glad to answer the phone until one of them arrives."

"Thanks, Tony. "I'll call back as soon as I know something."

"Are you going to be okay driving over there by yourself 'cause I can cancel my appointment," asked Lucinda.

"I'll be fine going by myself Lucinda. Don't worry. I'll call soon as I know anything."

When Brooksie drove up in front of Melissa's house she spotted Marino's car and he and his partner got out and walked over to her car.

"Hi Marino and Detective Swain. I'm sorry if I have called you for nothing, but Melissa never misses work. I pray this is a false alarm and I don't embarrass the hell out of Melissa."

Detective Swain responded, "Please call me Joe, it's not like we're strangers. Don't ever worry about looking foolish. It's always better to be safe than sorry. Anyway, Marino and I were both glad to get away from the paperwork piled sky-high on our desks."

The three walked up to the door and Brooksie knocked and called out, "Melisssa it's me Brooksie. I'm just making sure that all is okay. Hello Melissa, anybody home?"

There was no response to the bell ringing or knocking. No sound could be heard from inside the house.

Detective Swain looked into the garage window and saw that the car was inside. He then went around to the back of the house. Marino looked into the windows in the front and side of the house He started inspecting the area around the house.

Joe called to Marino to come around back and for Brooksie to go back to her car and wait.

Her heart started racing and she stammered "What's wrong? Is Melissa there? What's the problem Blake? Joe what's going on?"

"Go back to your car and wait for me," shouted Marino. His tone was deadly serious.

Minutes passed, but they seemed like hours to Brooksie. Finally, Marino walked slowly toward her car, head down and shoulders slumped forward. His body language was screaming bad news. He climbed into the passenger seat of Brooksie's car and told her that Melissa had apparently been shot and was dead. "It appears she has been dead for quite a while, probably since last night. The coroner and the crew will be here soon. I'm so sorry. I know that you were friends."

"Are you sure it's Melissa? Can I see her?" Her voice was choked with unreleased sobs. She let out one wail deep from within and quickly took several deep breaths to regain control of her emotions.

"No, you can't go in. Her place is a crime scene and you don't want to mess up any evidence. And yes I'm sure it's Melissa. I've seen her several times at the clinic's office."

"Where will they take her?" asked Brooksie.

"Hon, an autopsy will need to be done. Does she have any family?"

"I don't believe so. She left me a message last night from The Barn and said she had just seen someone having to do with one of our groups. She said she was going to double check the identity and let me know in the morning who it was. She asked to meet me at 7:30 a.m. at the office. If we had talked last night maybe this wouldn't have happened. Who could possibly have wanted to hurt her? She was a caring, great secretary and lover of life. She never talked about being afraid of anyone. Although last night she sounded different. She called and left me a message. I didn't get home till close to 9 p.m. because after finishing the divorce group at eight I stopped and shopped for pet food. I figured it was too late to call her back. The message Melissa left was about seeing someone at The Barn who she didn't think she was supposed to see.

"I need to call Lucinda and let the others know what has happened." Brooksie's chin began to quiver. She stopped talking, trying to maintain control, but without success. The dam broke and the tears flooded her eyes which she covered with her scarf, it was soon dripping wet. "How can this be? Is the clinic cursed, a magnet for murder? Who in the hell could have wanted to hurt Melissa?"

Detective Marino seemingly uncomfortable offered his sympathy and added, "Officer Lanson is going to take your statement after he drives you back to your office or if you feel you can drive, he will follow you to the clinic."

Brooksie red-eyed and pale said to the officer, "Please take me to the office so I can break the terrible news to my friends and then you can drive me to the precinct or not. I'll tell you what I know at either place. Will that be okay?"

Officer Lanson nodded in the affirmative. He helped slow moving Brooksie into the squad car and off they went to the clinic.

The crime scene officers got busy with their tasks. No gun or spent cartridges were found. She was apparently sleeping when an intruder shot her in the head. There were no defense wounds. Her cell phone was missing. Nothing else seemed out of order. The back door was unlocked.

The police car pulled up at the clinic parking lot. Brooksie sat for a minute. Her legs refusing to cooperate as if they had suddenly become paralyzed. Shock had rendered her temporarily immobilized. The officer stood by the door not knowing what he should do. Should he pick her up, pull her to her feet or call for help? He gently pulled her to her feet and she slowly made her way to the office door with the kind officer's assistance. She blew her nose, did some deep breathing and stood tall like a statue as she entered the building.

Lucinda was sitting in Melissa's chair talking on the phone. She looked up and saw a pale-faced, red-eyed Brooksie leaning on the arm of a policeman. It looked like he was keeping her from falling over. She immediately ended the phone call. "What is it Brooksie? What's happened? Oh my God, it's bad news."

Lucinda rushed across the room and hugged Brooksie very tightly. Lucinda immediately began to cry. The two held each other crying while Brooksie, between sobs, shared the horrible news.

Rachael and Tony, hearing the commotion, came to the front office. Brooksie again gave a short report about the murder of

Melissa. She then turned to the officer and told him she was ready to go and give her limited information. Lucinda asked if she could also go. The others stayed at the office. Rachael offered to notify the psychologist and cancel all of the appointments for Don, Lucinda and her own for today. Brooksie usually had no appointments on Fridays. This being Friday, the office would be closed for the weekend. Each staff member would then have to make their own plans for the following week.

After Brooksie and Lucinda left with the officer, Rachael said to Don and Tony, "What the shit is happening? We may need to rename the clinic the death clinic. That sounded awful. I'm sorry I'm scared and worried for all of us. This is tearing Brooksie apart. She is so sensitive to the anguish and suffering of others. She befriends everyone she meets. She often complimented Melissa and thanked her for all she did in the office. Who for God's sake would want to hurt Melissa? She always had a smile on her face and had an upbeat attitude. We never know if we will see the sun come up tomorrow."

CHAPTER ELEVEN

The presence of that absence is everywhere.
Edna St. Vincent Millay

Brooksie and Lucinda arrived at the police station. Mascara stained Lucinda's face and both women exit the car in zombie-like fashion. Officer Larson shows them to a small room. Detective Marino and Detective Swain follow close behind.

Another officer enters with a recorder and notepad.

Marino began, "This is just a formality. I'll be waiting outside for you to finish and drive you back to the office.

"Is it okay if Lucinda stays with me?" asked Brooksie. Her eyes were puffy and the end of her nose was reddened from much use of tissue. Her hair looked like it had been arranged by her pets.

Detective Marino responded, "No problem. Sorry to ask you to do this now, but some of the details are fresh in your mind and if we wait very long, some might just slip away. Take a few deep breaths, relax as best you can and tell officer Markson all you can remember, starting with Melissa's message last night."

Brooksie related all she could about the call, the time, the exact words for the most part and the strangeness in Melissa's voice. She told the officer that Shaun was Melissa's date and a fairly new boyfriend. She asked if Shaun was notified and in the same breath asked if he was a suspect. The officer stated that when

Shaun had been told about Melissa's death he yelled at the officer and said, 'You must have made a mistake. I was just with her last night.' He looked dazed, his eyes were blank and he became unsteady on his feet and one of the officers had to help him sit down. After a few minutes he asked if we could call his friend Pete to pick him up because he didn't feel he was okay to drive. He was white as a sheet and asked repeatedly if we were sure it was Melissa."

Brooksie's interview was over in less than fifteen minutes. The two women were dismissed and Marino drove them back to the office. When they arrived her car she had left at Melissa's was parked in the lot and the car keys were in her office.

After some discussion, Rachael and Tony agreed to share Melissa's desk duties for the following week. Brooksie said she would contact the employment service next Monday and try to at least hire a temporary secretary until more permanent plans could be made.

The next hour was spent talking about Melissa's demise. Everyone had a chance to vent their mixed bag of emotions. Brooksie took on the job of looking for any relatives of Melissa. Don and Rachael would look into funeral arrangements. Lucinda and Tony offered to figure out Melissa's billing system and talk with the accountant.

Dr. Charlene Jackson, the psychologist who had replaced Dr. Primm, walked into the front office as the five were finishing up making plans for the next week or so. Rachael broke the news to Dr. Jackson. "I must admit, I'm beginning to feel some concern for safety at this clinic. Are any precautions being taken by the staff or for the clients?" She looked sternly at Rachael and asked if she also had any safety concerns for staff members.

Rachael answered, "Absolutely not." This was said to convince herself. "Common sense dictates when leaving the office at night to be sure to walk in pairs to your respective cars. Most of us have finished with groups or individual clients by eight p.m. So there is a number of people in the parking area at the same time."

"Sounds like a good plan. I'll do the same," responded Dr. Jackson.

Dr. Jackson offered to take care of making her own appointments until a temp could be hired and she volunteered to lock up the office with another staff member at 8 p.m. weeknights.

After little discussion, the rest of the staff agreed to meet at Brooksie's house around 6 p.m. Rachael and Don would pick up pizza and Brooksie would furnish the drinks. They all seemed to feel the need to rally around each other, sort of like circling the wagons. Maybe for comfort or for safety. There was an unspoken sense of a nameless danger.

Dr. Jackson asked if she could be included.

Several said they would be glad to have her presence there. Don offered to bring her in his car and would later return her to the office to pick up her car.

"Since I'm retiring next month, I want to do as many good deeds as possible. I hope to be missed," said Don. Wearing a big smile.

She politely declined his offer of transportation, but asked for directions to Brooksie's house, which she received from Lucinda.

That evening the sad and somewhat frightened group gathered at Brooksie's home. After the greetings, hugs and questions were thrown about and left with no answers, the pizza was passed around.

Brooksie's pet companions were busily sniffing and pleading with upturned soft eyes for any kind of morsel. Preferring, of course, the sausage from the piazza. Gandhi and Sugar both leaned on Brooksie. It was as if they were trying to offer comfort to their beloved keeper. Dogs, more so than cats, seem to sense the moods of their owners. They offer comfort without saying a word.

Dr. Jackson showed up a half-hour later and said, "I didn't know Melissa very well, but I had just joined the Oceanside Gym and ran into her. She was also a new member of the gym. We chatted a few times while we both huffed and puffed on the treadmills. She was very friendly and likeable. Do they have any suspects yet?"

Brooksie answered, "Not that we know about. None of us were very close to Melissa. She was a great secretary and was always in a good mood. She's been with the clinic ever since it opened. Her violent death makes no sense what so ever. Too many deaths connected to the clinic. Why?"

The room remained silent for a long minute.

Lucinda broke the silence, "Does anyone have any ideas or knowledge of Melissa's private life? I don't have a clue. She never acted out of sorts, worried or frightened on my watch."

There was a general consensus that Melissa kept her private life to herself. There didn't seem to be any family or even close friends that she ever talked about. The discussion turned to their own feelings and fears about the number of deaths connected to the clinic. Then all agreed they were tired and it was time to go home. Brooksie restated she would locate a temporary worker and put out a feeler for a permanent secretary. Others in the group would work on a memorial after obtaining feedback from Shaun, her boyfriend.

CHAPTER TWELVE

**You get treated in life the way
you train people to treat you.**
Dr. Robert Anthony - *Think Again*

Lucinda and Tony are on their way to her mother's house for dinner. It was Wednesday evening. They had many discussions about keeping either the dinner date or cancelling it because of Melissa's death. Since the funeral wouldn't be for several more days, they agreed to go ahead with the planned dinner. Lucinda was as nervous as a first time mother in labor. Her mother was not the kind of mother to receive the Mother-of-the-Year award . any time soon, for sure not in this century.

Tony picked up Lucinda because she wanted them to arrive together and be able to leave at the same time. She told him the dress code was very casual and gave him her address, which was close to the clinic.

"I told my mother I was bringing a friend along for dinner. At first she didn't say anything. It took her so long to respond. I thought she had hung up on me. Mom finally said ever so sweetly, 'I'm glad to meet someone you work with.' If she mouths off to you, please don't take it personally."

"Lucinda, I'm not made of glass. Please don't worry about my feelings. I've had plenty of experience with difficult people.

"By the way, why is your mother's last name different from yours?"

"Mom reverted back to her family name after dad walked out on her. I had two short-term failed marriages and always kept my dad's name of Chavez. I loved my dad and he was good to me. I've always felt more like a Chavez than a Reicht. Plus it pisses mom off that I kept his name."

They pulled up in Mrs. Reicht's driveway and Lucinda took a few deep breaths. "I'm as ready as I'm going to be. Let's roll."

Tony says, "That sounds as if we are heading into a war zone."

"We are, except this time I brought reinforcements."

Mrs. Reicht had been busy preparing her favorite meal of pot roast, boiled potatoes, cucumber and onion salad with sour cream and warm spicy red cabbage. She thought to herself, *I know Lucy hates red cabbage, says it gives her gas. Too bad, it's my house and my kitchen and my groceries.*

Lucinda rang the doorbell, her hands shook like someone with palsy. Mrs. Reicht opened the door and bellowed out, "I have to cook a fantastic meal to get you to come to see me Lucy."

"Hello to you too, Mom," responded Lucinda. "This is Tony Padilla. He is a volunteer facilitator at the clinic."

"Oh, so you are unemployed?" asked Lucinda's mother.

"Nice to meet you Mrs. Reicht," responded Tony and shook her hand firmly. "No, I'm not unemployed. I volunteer at the clinic a few hours a week, work at home in my cabinet shop and also write books."

"I didn't know you were a cabinet maker and an author. What kind of books do you write?" asked Lucinda.

"Children's books and instructional books about cabinetry."

"So, are you famous or something?" asked Mrs. Reicht.

"No ma'am, but I thoroughly enjoy my work and it keeps the bills paid for my daughter and me."

Lucinda asked, "Mom, can I do anything to help you get the food on the table?"

"No. I have everything ready. You two sit down, pour some wine and I'll bring in the roast. Everything else is already on the table. Have you so quickly forgotten what an organized person I am? Not that you got any of my cooking or organizational skills.

"Your dad was always so disorganized. Even he had to admit I could make the best enchiladas, better than his own Mexican mother. She didn't like me much. She was jealous that her son liked my Mexican food better than his own mother's cooking. That's okay, I didn't like her either."

Tony added, "Everything smells and looks great. I haven't had a home cooked meal in a long time. This is a real treat for me. I do the cooking for Katrina, I'm not very creative."

"I take it you are not married or living with some woman?"

"No," answered Tony." I have no special lady in my life. Katrina's mother died a few years ago."

"I wouldn't set your cap for Lucy. She messes up all relationships. She can't seem to keep a man around, even chased off her own father," said Mrs. Reicht.

"Mom, are you really going to start off bad mouthing me so soon. You invited me and a friend for dinner. I was hoping for a pleasant experience and for decent conversation. I've had one sip of wine and just about to have my first bite of this good looking meal and you start in with ugly talk."

Mrs. Reicht began passing the various dishes of food around to Tony. "You take everything so serious. You are going to make Tony uncomfortable. Pass the potatoes and cabbage."

Everyone fills their plates and only the sound of chewing is heard for the next few minutes.

"Lucy you didn't take any cabbage it's one of my specialties," remarked Mrs. Reicht.

"Everything is fabulous mom. Cabbage and I don't like each other, but of course you know that."

Mrs. Reicht with her mouth half full, speaks out, "Sure is nice having someone to cook for and have dinner with. My daughter doesn't come around to see if I'm okay. I have to leave notes on her door to get her to even call me even once in a great while. I could be dead on the floor and no one would find my body for weeks.

"Tony, do you have parents living nearby?"

"No. My dad died a few years back and mom lives in Tacoma in the family home. My sister, Rosa, lives a block from her."

Mrs. Reicht said, "I bet you visit her often. She is lucky to have you and your sister."

"Actually, I don't visit her, but once or twice a year. She is very difficult to be around. My sister checks on her once in a while. They don't get along either. My mother is a whiner and a blamer. She drove my dad crazy with her mean tongue and her constant complaining.

"By the way, this roast and everything else is delicious. This kind of salad is new to me. I really like it! Can I pour anyone more wine?"

Mrs. Reicht is staring at her half-empty glass. Her nose and cheeks are turning a reddish color and her respirations are loud enough to be heard at a football game. Her eyeballs are barely peeking out from her half closed eyelids. She bellows out, "Now I know why you brought him here. He hates his mother too. I can see right through the both of you."

Lucinda nearly knocks her chair over when she leaps up. "Mom, I don't hate you. I do hate the way you talk to me and the horrible way you talked to dad. It's the awful things you say to most everyone. You drive me and others away with your meanness. You invited me and my friend to dinner. In my heart I was hoping you wanted to have me back in your life and you were going to treat me with respect and kindness. No! That is not why you asked me to come here. You refuse to accept responsibility for the poisonous words you spit out at all who come in contact with you. No more! I'm done being your whipping post. I will never again listen to your nastiness, your hatefulness and your blaming me for what you've created for yourself.

"Tony please take me home."

As soon as Tony helped Lucinda into his car, she apologized for her mother's behavior and for ruining his evening.

Tony responded, "No need to apologize for someone else's behavior. Your mother is the only one responsible for what escapes her mouth. I am most impressed with your handling of her the time we were there. In my humble opinion, your last statement to your mom, was both truthful and factual, and in the long run, very kind. She can replay the information and make constructive changes or not, her choice. You gave her a solution to her loneliness. At this moment you may be sad and hurting, but I feel you performed a loving and a brave act.

"How would you like to stop somewhere for coffee and dessert before I take you home?"

"I would like that. Thanks for going with me into the lions' den. I have mixed emotions. I'm sad, angry and disappointed because of the way my mother acts the way she does, but I also feel relief. To be completely honest, I feel, "Free at last," quoting Martin Luther King.

Tony pulled into a parking space at the Table Talk Cafe. They went inside and sat down in a corner booth.

Lucinda stated, "I know very little about you. I don't want to pry, but I am interested in why you volunteer at the clinic. I didn't even know you had a daughter until tonight."

"I'll be happy to give you a short version of my not very exciting life. When I see your eyes begin to glaze over I promise I will stop.

"First, let me tell you why I volunteer. It's because I have seen the effects of long term grief. My brother died in a car accident years ago. My dad was the driver and he never got over his guilt or grief. My Mom used the accident to torture dad on a daily basis. It was simply an accident on a very rainy day, wet street and poor visibility. Dad swerved to miss an animal and lost control of the car.

"Secondly, was my ten year marriage to Julianna. She became increasingly depressed after only a few years of being married. Along came Katrina, our beautiful baby girl, and it was downhill emotionally for Julianna soon after the birth. She became practically incapacitated. And I became progressively more concerned for Katrina's safety because her mother's behavior was unpredictable. I could not leave Katrina alone for fear her mother would forget to feed her, change her diaper or the very worst that she would let her drown while giving the baby a bath.

"Eventually, Julianna was committed to a state hospital and started to receive medication on a regular basis. Once improved and discharged I rented her an apartment near us. I couldn't jeopardize Katrina's safety by allowing her mother to live under the same roof. Julianna's parents were a great help to me and their granddaughter. I divorced Julianna four years ago. She committed suicide three years ago. At times I struggle with guilt about her suicide, but I know deep down I did my best to get her help. Then there comes the guilt because I felt such relief that Julianna's confusion and pain were over and my fears for my daughter had also ceased.

"Katrina is magnificent and we have a great life. In the beginning, I needed to take full time care of my child. That is where my cabinet shop and my writing started. Katrina seems to love to make things in my shop. She also will write little stories when I'm banging away on the computer. My stories are for children and about their innate curiosities and strengths.

"So, there you have my life in a nutshell. Now it is your turn."

"I'm very moved by the care and love you have shown to your daughter. Thank you for letting me get to know you a little better. I would rather take a rain check and be the one to ask you to go for coffee and dessert and tell you my story. Would that be okay with you?"

"Sounds like a great idea. You have a date."

CHAPTER THIRTEEN

**The strongest principle of growth
lies in the human choice.**
George Eliot
Daniel Deronda

Session Four

The three group facilitators were drinking coffee in Brooksie's office discussing the divorce group. The meeting was due to begin in less than an hour.

"What are we going to say about Melissa to anyone tonight if someone should ask why she wasn't at her desk?" asked Tony.

"Our wonderful secretary of almost five years has died. The circumstances of her death are not clear, but it was not a natural death. The police are involved and are keeping us informed. We are all very sad and still in shock. She died last Thursday night and the memorial will be held tomorrow," suggested Brooksie.

"That sounds okay to me. Since she has already been cremated we are just having a sort of a farewell service, right?" asked Lucinda.

"Yes," answered Brooksie. "Her boyfriend Shaun wanted her service to take place at the beach. He has taken possession of her ashes. Melissa didn't have any living relatives. Everyone from the clinic may be going and I've invited Anita and Brad. Anita responded they are coming. Makes me sad to think Melissa had no family except for all of us at the office and Shaun, of course.

"Before the group members get here I would like to ask how did the dinner at your mom's house go?"

Lucinda answered, "It seems so trivial now, but I will say mom was a bitch. She wouldn't control her nasty mouth. She was rude to Tony and insulting to me. Tony was a gentleman and a saint. She belittled me and did her best to make me feel sorry for her, at the same time. She likes to embarrass me in front of any and all. Tony was gracious and tried to change the subject by sincerely complimenting her cooking. Flattery didn't faze her. She asked him about his own mother and he told her that he seldom visits his mother in Tacoma because she chooses to whine, complain, and say hurtful things about everyone, especially him and his sister and himself. Actually his mother sounds like a clone of my mom.

"Mom followed up with, 'Now I know why you brought him. You both hate your mothers.'

I told her I don't hate her, but I do hate the poisonous words she routinely spits at me. I'm through allowing her the opportunity to beat me up verbally. I feel rotten to say this, but I'm so relieved that I don't need to have anything to do with her anymore."

"I'm sorry your mother is so screwed up and hateful," commented Brooksie. "She's the loser. What you said to her sounded like it was from your heart and actually very kind. Once again, You have given her choices, continue to spit out venom or make nice. You have no control over what she says or does. You have no responsibility for her meanness.

"Sounds like you and Tony have something in common. Two messed-up mothers."

Lucinda added, "I'm so grateful Tony went with me to mom's house of horrors." At this point in the conversation Lucinda displayed a Cheshire cat smile, grinning from ear to ear. Her cheeks began to glow and her eyes sparkled like polished gems. "I admit I feel relieved, almost euphoric, like a heavy boulder has been removed off of my heart.

"I hear others coming, we had better walk over to the group room."

The group members began to file in just as Lucinda finished her story. Brooksie and Lucinda moved swiftly in order to greet the members at the entrance to the room.   Tony was the last one to enter He winked at Lucinda. Lucinda quickly looked at Brooksie to see if she had noticed the wink, but Brooksie pretended not to notice.

"Good day to you all. We will begin again by asking if anyone has something they feel they would like to share about last week."

Jason quickly spoke up, "Yes. I briefly want to report that Loreli is still acting and looking very unhappy. I offered to take her to a counselor of her choice, but she refuses. I worry about her when I'm not at home. Also, off the subject of Loreli, I wondered if Melissa was sick. She wasn't at her desk this evening."

Lucinda takes a quick peek at Brooksie.

"I am very sad to tell you all that Melissa died last Thursday night. The police are involved, but so far we only have a few details to share. I can say it was not a natural death. She was shot while she was sleeping," responded Brooksie.

Dead silence in the room. Someone gasped and Melika reached for the tissue box.

"You mean she was murdered?" asked Kent.

"That is what the police have told us," said Brooksie. "We are going to continue with our group for tonight. I know you are all shocked by this terrible news and we will stick around after the meeting for a few minutes if any of you want to talk more about Melissa."

Lucinda asked, "Jason you were talking about Loreli. Could one of her friends stay with her when you are elsewhere?"

"I've suggested that, but she gets angry. She accuses me of not trusting her and wanting to hire a babysitter just to humiliate her."

Brooksie asked, "Does she have any family that might be able to help out?"

Jason responded, "No. She has no living relatives. At least that is what she's told me."

"How about contacting a family doctor? Someone must have prescribed the pills she takes. The ones you told us about," asked Cecelia.

"I can try that again, maybe she will agree to see a doctor. Thank you all for your concern and suggestions."

Brooksie announced, "I'm going to use the blackboard again. The topic is specific challenges. For example, children, custody concerns, finances, work-related difficulties, role changes, loneliness, and whatever else you might think about. We will choose one topic to begin with. Everyone can throw out a word or two of whatever comes to mind."

Melika spoke first, "One of my concerns is definitely my children. I know not everyone in this group has kids, but maybe we could look at this subject for a moment."

"What word or words come to mind Melika?"asked Lucinda.

"Lies that my ex tells our children mainly to hurt me, but they also hurt and confuse the kids," responded Melika.

Jason offered, "Unfaithfulness. How is that explained to a child?"

"Secrets. How much and when should a child be told?" said Cecelia.

Ruth mumbled under her breath, "Taking sides."

"I would like to add my own two cents," said Lucinda. "Guilt, intimidation, manipulation and selfishness of a parent."

Brooksie added her word, bribes to the board.

The last one to speak up was Kent. His contribution were the words shame and paying a price for the behaviors of the parents.

"Let's sum up the words I have written on the board," said Brooksie. "Lies, negativity, explaining unfaithfulness to children, secrets from children, taking sides, blaming the kids for parents behaviors, guilt, intimidation, manipulation, bribery, shame and consequences."

Lucinda took over, "First off, the age and maturity of a child is an important factor in what, when, and how detailed should be the deciding factor in giving information to the child. The motive of the parent or parents, the timing and the tone of voice used are other considerations."

Brooksie continued, "Here are a few suggestions. Some of these are for those of you that have small children or grown up ones.

- Remind the children frequently that they are loved and are lovable.
- Be clear as to motive when giving information.
- Secrets don't work, but timing is important. Can anyone of you think about a secret that may be hurting your child or hurting another adult?
- Start with few facts and build the information up slowly based on the individual.
- Always keep in mind the level of understanding of the child before passing on information.
- A child is never to blame for the parents' mistakes and poor decisions.

Brooksie asked Melika, "Have you heard anything that might apply to you and your children?"

"Yes. The words to do with secrets, age appropriate and mature touch a nerve with me."

Ruth spoke up, "Why shouldn't older kids take sides?"

Tony answered, "Because they are not responsible for the problems. To make a child, at any age, choose between a parent is cruel and damaging. It is the parents who bear total responsibility for their own relationship."

"That's for sure. I didn't realize for a long time how horrible my parents really were. What a horrible and embarrassing, childhood I had to live through. In fact, I'm just now coming to grips with that," added Kent.

Shannon responded, "It makes me sad to think about the pain my ex and I have caused our son. Our marriage was lousy almost from the beginning. Somewhere down deep in my heart I knew my young son felt my sadness. I allowed him to witness my husband's meanness. I wonder if my son felt responsible for the misery in our home.

"I know I can't change the past, but I'm going to make sure no one ever gets a second chance to belittle or intimidate me. I want to show Brodie, my son, that marriage or commitment to one person can be a great adventure filled with joy, laughter, kindness and even challenges."

"I think a parent who brings disgrace to his kids and causes them to feel shame should be sent to jail along with the mother who allows her husband to cause such emotional and financial damage to the innocent ones," replied Kent with both fists clenched.

"For fear of sounding radical, I not only agree with you Kent, but I would want parents who display outrageous behaviors to receive much harsher consequences." Jason continued, "Not so long ago, and even today in some countries, an adulteress is stoned

CHAPTER FOURTEEN

**To disagree, one doesn't have
to be disagreeable.**
Barry Goldwater

Marino arrived at Brooksie's home, parked his 1957 Corvette in the driveway and strolled to the door. Before he had a chance to knock, Brooksie opened the door. She greeted him with an ear to ear smile and a wet kiss.

"If your mom and sister weren't waiting, I'd let you fling me over your shoulder and head for the bedroom. I've missed you."

"I've missed you too. Thanks for going with me all the way to Olympia to meet them. They are both anxious to get acquainted with you. I especially appreciate it, since the death of Melissa. A change of routine may be good for you.

"They can't wait to tell you what a terrible kid I was when I was little. I hope you don't get bothered by all the questions they will ask. They're both nosy, but harmless and very Italian. Mom will keep pushing food on your plate and she will keep it coming until you think you might burst. Again, that is simply Italian hospitality.

"This past week has been a bear. I've been assigned two new cases on top of what was already in the mix. I'm still working on last month's homicides."

"Is there any connection between Melissa's death and the cases you have been working on?" asked Brooksie.

"So far, hon, we have no suspect in Melissa's case or in the others. The department has many staff members working on her case and believe me, we won't leave any stone unturned. Just like last year, every staff member will have to be interviewed. This investigation is a number one priority for me and the other homicide detectives."

"An investigator came to the clinic asking about one of the clients in a divorce group. Would it be possible for you to check out the investigator?"

"Sure. I'll have Ronda do a little snooping tomorrow. Let's get a move on. My Mom hates for us to be late and I hate it when she gives me her down-the-nose look. Reminds me of when I was a little guy and having to always do what I was told. My dad was the dictator type and my mom was the bossy type about whatever went on in the home."

"I see where you get your strong personality," said Brooksie.

He smiled. "Guess so."

"While we're talking about personalities," Brooksie said as they started their drive, "I'd like to ask your opinion of a problem we're having at work."

"Go ahead. I'm all ears."

"The private investigator I just told you about, Mr. Edwards, asked if we could meet so he could give me some information about a possible client. I met with him and he shared some disturbing, so called facts, about one of the members of my present divorce group. The member in question states he is separated and wants to reunite with his spouse, who is apparently a very wealthy woman. There is a question about his past and previous marriage to another wealthy woman. She died under questionable and strange circumstances. There is also a question about his name change.

"My concern is about the safety of his wife. Maybe I'm overreacting because of the previous homicides, or I'm becoming paranoid, suspicious and completely out of touch with reality. My gut instincts are a mess and no longer trustworthy. Do you have any ideas?"

Marino answered, "Have you spoken to the clinic's attorney?"

"Yes, he suggested waiting for one or two more group sessions to see if this person brings up his previous marriage and name change."

Marino responded, "Let me check out the investigator. I can quickly see if he is on the up and up. Your clinic is beginning to sound like a hot bed of criminal activity. Maybe you should have a cop on the payroll. I'd volunteer my services, but guarding you would not be one of them. I would have other jobs in mind concerning you that have nothing at all to do with police work."

Several hours later, the Corvette pulled into a tree-lined driveway which was next to a two-story clapboard house. It was painted white with dark green trim. A petite, attractive young woman waved enthusiastically from a large inviting front porch.

Blake smiled as they approached. "Hi Sis! This is Brooksie, Brooksie this is my sister, Rafael. Blake and Rafael bear hug and the three of them go inside. They find Mrs. Marino in the kitchen with a colorful apron covering most of her abundant frame. A mix of wonderful smells, garlic being the dominate one, permeated the air. She greeted Brooksie in a warm embrace then whisked them all into the dining room.

Blake rolled his eyes. "Mom, you didn't give me time to introduce Brooksie. Mom, this is Brooksie and Brooksie this is Marcella."

"Please call me Marcie, Brooksie. Dinner is ready. We can get better acquainted after we eat."

"We have to get back soon, Mom." Blake added. "We both have early commitments tomorrow." Blake winked at Brooksie, who blushed and looked down at her plate.

"I have heard about your fantastic cooking Mrs. Marino, oops, Marcie," corrected Brooksie.

"I do pride myself on my cooking," Marcie said.

The delicious meal was soon finished and the short, but friendly conversation drew to an end. Blake gave his mom and sis kisses and said it was time to go. Brooksie was also treated to hugs by both women and their wishes to see her again in the near future.

After, he parked in his driveway Marino said, "I hope you are ready to make good the promise you made when you opened the door."

As they walked up to the house, Brooksie asked, "What promise would that be detective?"

"It was made and sealed with a long, deep and wet kiss and now I plan to collect just to keep you honest," answered Marino.

"I'd never deceive a policeman. I wouldn't want you to arrest me and force you, in the line of duty, to use your handcuffs." She displayed a wide grin and with a twinkle in her eyes.

CHAPTER FIFTEEN

**Animals are such agreeable friends - they
ask no questions, they pass no criticisms.**
George Eliot - Scenes of Clerical Life

It's Sunday afternoon and Brooksie was making last minute preparations to go to Aunt Tilly and Uncle Joe's mini ranch for their monthly dinner. She loaded the car with the two new cat beds and forty pounds of dry cat food for her family's every growing pet population. Before leaving, she checked the water supply for her pets and made sure their food dishes were filled to the brim, locked the door and off she went.

Half an hour later she arrived at the entrance to their property. A rambling, gravel road filled with some seriously deep pot holes.

Brooksie received a warm greeting by a variety of dogs and cats. Some tails moving like metronomes and others like windmills. Every critter seemed happy to see her, especially attentive to whatever she usually held in her pockets. Treats are passed throughout the menagerie and the crunching of bones and fish cookies being chewed are the only sounds. The contented scene is loudly interrupted by Waldo, an oversized St. Bernard who came bounding from behind the house and said his slobbery hello.

"Waldo," yelled Uncle Joe. "Brooksie, stand your ground or you will become one more victim of this giant love machine. He has no understanding of his size and weight and absolutely no manners."

"Hi Uncle Joe. Hold on a minute Waldo. I have to have enough room to get your bone out of my pocket, you big ox."

Waldo was surprisingly gentle about taking the offered treat. He made a quick retreat to his favorite spot at the bottom of the steps and began to noisily chomp away on Brooksie's gift.

Inside, Brooksie gave her aunt a big hug. Then they all sat down for dinner.

"Now what's this about your secretary getting herself murdered?" Her aunt asked.

Brooksie began telling them the few known details about Melissa's death. She reassured them that no staff members were in danger, hoping to make herself believe the same. Her own doubts crept in of late. *Perhaps all of us at the clinic need to start taking precautions. Or maybe I'm just letting my imagination run wild.*

"Maybe I need to find you a guard dog," said Aunt Tilly.

"No. I think Melissa saw something or someone she wasn't supposed to. If I get any more dogs I'll need a license to run a shelter. So, thanks for the concern, but no guard dog. If you don't mind, I would rather not think about poor Melissa today. Please bring me up to date on your rescue operations."

Uncle Joe proudly spoke of the seven dogs and four cats his wife had found loving homes for, this past month alone.

"You're an amazing woman, Auntie." Brooksie looked over at Uncle Joe and inquired, "I'm wondering if you know of a landscaper or gardener to hire. My back yard is simply too much for me to take care of. It looks like a hurricane recently visited. I need someone with good, practical ideas that would be willing to keep up the front and back yard, at least once a month or more often, if necessary."

"I know just the person. His name is Luke Jones," responded Uncle Joe.

"That's right," added Tilly. "He's very talented and works for several families we know. Their yards are absolutely beautiful. I'll give you his phone number before you leave today. He's not bad looking either and he has graciously accepted two old rescue dogs and two adorable kittens from us." She grinned.

"Now my dear Auntie, I'm not looking for a blind date. I just need some help with my yard. I'll call."

After they sat a spell, Brooksie gathered her purse and sweater, "My thanks again for a fantastic meal. But mostly for your love and kindness. I always feel renewed and rejuvenated after a visit with the two of you ." She hugged them both, petted the many furry bodies near her and got into her car. Before starting the engine, she called out to her aunt, "Do I have to check my car for any added passengers?"

"No dear. Not this time. Let us know how it turns out with Mr. Jones. And keep us informed about Melissa's murder."

Brooksie nodded in the affirmative and off she went, slowly down pothole alley.

CHAPTER SIXTEEN

**Certain things catch your eye, but pursue
only those that capture the heart.**
Ancient Indian Proverb

Brooksie dialed Mr. Jones' number. After four rings a voice sounding very young, almost elf-like, answered.

"Hi. Who are you."

Brooksie responded, "My name is Brooksie. Could you get Mr. Jones or your dad for me?"

She heard some papers rustling in the background, then she heard the sound of the receiver dropping. The tiny voice called for dad, and eventually a deep baritone voice responded, "Tell them I'll be right there."

A short time later she heard, "Hello, this is Luke Jones."

"Hello Mr. Jones. I'm sorry if I am calling at an inconvenient time. My name is Brooksie Everett and my Aunt Tilly and Uncle Joe suggested I call you."

"They told me you might call today. Sorry about my pee wee secretary dropping the phone. You just can't get a great assistant from preschool these days."

Brooksie laughed loudly, "No problem. I would like to make an appointment with you to come to my house to look at my yard.

I'm hoping you can make my backyard more suitable for pets, as well as, more inviting for two-legged creatures at the same time."

"Would Monday afternoon be okay?"

"Yes, but it would have to be after 6. I won't be leaving work until 5:30," answered Brooksie.

"I'll be at your house soon after 6. What is the address?"

"That would be perfect." Brooksie gave him her address and directions plus her phone number and after good-byes, hung up.

Immediately after putting the phone down, it rang. Brooksie hesitated before she picked up the receiver, she feared more bad news; which was a knee jerk reaction since the death of Melissa. Marino was on the other end of the line.

"Hi Brooksie. Marino here. How about a movie tonight? I thought you might need a distraction from what's going on around your clinic. I'll even let you do the picking. If you can behave yourself in a dark theater, I'll treat you to a soda afterwards."

"Sounds great Blake, but I just got home from my aunt's house. It's pretty late and I'm worn out. Thanks for thinking about me. I think I'm still in shock about Melissa. I can't imagine anyone wanting to hurt her, let alone kill her. I keep doing the 'what if' exercise. If only she had told me who she had seen that night. Maybe there is a connection. Do you have any leads as to a suspect yet?"

"No. So far no fingerprints have been identified because the perpetrator was wearing gloves. We have talked to Shaun because he was the last person to see her alive besides the killer, of course. He seemed pretty shaken up, but some of the worst people are the best actors."

Brooksie asked, "What about The Barn? There must have been someone there that night who Melissa recognized. That person must be connected some way to the clinic. I just assumed she meant someone from the clinic since she said I would be so surprised."

"Investigating all leads is a long and tedious process. I don't have anything new to share. The Barn is being checked out. Following up on all possible leads takes time and manpower. Now I'm even more on edge. I'm concerned about you and your staff's safety. Wish I could wave a magic wand and all the thieves and murderers would walk into the police station, turn themselves in and sign a confession. That's just not going to happen, hon. So while we are waiting for a miracle, how about we see a movie Wednesday night? What time should I pick you up?"

"How about 6:30? And thanks."

"You have yourself a date sweetie. By the way, I had your private investigator checked out. He is on the up and up. In fact, he is well known in his field as a man of integrity. He has built a damn good reputation for his work."

"Thanks for the information. It will help me and the other facilitators clear up some discrepancies and maybe even some safety issues."

"You're not playing detective again are you? Don't forget the lessons you were supposed to learn with your psychologist friend Sharon the mercy killer."

"Marino, Sharon is a woman of honor and courage. I haven't forgotten about what she did and why she felt she had to do it. I admire her and hope to work with her at the prison."

"Let's not go there. You know how I feel about the way you place yourself in danger. At this rate, the clinic is keeping my department busy, and before you even go there, the clinic is not cursed! You are naïve when it comes to the dark side of people. I've worked with scum for years. My father died trying to protect someone like you, someone completely trusting."

"You're right. Let's not go there. I don't think we will ever agree on this subject. Let's just agree to disagree," replied Brooksie. *I don't know how long I can do this. He's not going to change and I don't want to. I love my job. If we married I would disappear into his life. What am I going to do?*

"Brooksie I won't change my mind on this. See you Wednesday. Maybe you can find us a good movie?"

CHAPTER SEVENTEEN

**"I'm happier because I made up
my mind to be that way."**
Merle Haggard

It was 6 p.m. exactly and Brooksie heard what sounded like a shotgun firing. She looked out the front room window and watched the approaching of an old beat up truck coming up the driveway. She walked out to meet Mr. Jones and observed the back of the truck. It was filled to overflowing with ladders, mowers, pots of bushes and an assortment of gardening tools.

A tall, tanned and well toned man emerged from this antique of a truck. The most noticeable feature of the man was his smile; which stretched from ear to ear showing off his sparkling white teeth. The two top teeth were slightly separated adding even more interest to his smile. He was sporting a crew cut and was clean shaven. He extended his paw-sized hand to envelope Brooksie's much smaller hand. She could feel his numerous calluses when they shook hands. She thought to herself, *a handshake can say a lot about a person and this man is gentle and strong at the same time.*

"This is a fine looking place you have here Miss Everett. I'd like to look over the backyard first, if you don't mind."

She walked him through the house on the way to the back patio. Mr. Jones received the usual "dog sniff" greeting from all six dogs plus the two cats named Samson and his shadow Sox. Samson was a cat who hadn't yet figured out to what species he belonged. Actually, Samson acted more like a dog in cat's clothing. Sox simply loved Samson and the dogs and would seek attention from all, day and night.

Mr. Jones patiently puts up with the crotch salute and gently pats each one of his greeters. Samson and Sox are both weaving in and out of Mr. Jones's legs. He picks both up, scratches them under their furry necks and returns them to the ground, all in one slow motion.

Mr. Jones asked, "So how many of these animals are gifts from your aunt?"

"All of them, I think of them more like mandatory adoptees though. I do love and cherish each one, but my aunt is manically persuasive. She will stop at nothing in order to obtain a loving home for one of her waifs. She is a woman on a mission. A woman I greatly admire.

"I understand she has used her wiles on you as well. How many do you feed every day?"

"I think your aunt has taken a little pity on me. I only have two dogs, Jack and Jill, and two cats so named Cinnamon and Sugar. All were named by Joel. You met Joel on the phone yesterday, my pee wee assistant. He is four going on fifteen. He hasn't been with me very long so he's not quite housebroken. Time to get to work."

Brooksie led him through the living room then onto the patio area.

"Wow, this is a fine back yard. It looks to be about one acre with a two magnificent sycamore trees. I can see it is quite a handful for you, but you've done a good job of working with nature."

While they walked around, Mr. Jones wrote down some notes and drew a few sketches.

"I can have a preliminary design ready in three days of suggested ideas for your backyard. How about I come back around 7 p.m., three days from now?"

"Mr. Jones, I have to work late on Thursday night. I wouldn't be home until after 7:30. How about Friday at 5:30 p.m.? Unless you already have plans."

"No plans for me for Friday. I'll be here at 5:30 p.m.," "How about you call me Luke? That sounds friendlier."

"Okay Luke, if you will call me Brooksie?"

Brooksie took notice that Luke smelled of freshly cut grass, clean dirt and baled hay. A very pleasant smell.

"You've got a deal, Brooksie."

Brooksie wanted to follow up with questions about Joel, but got the feeling Jones had said all he wanted to about his little boy.

"Thanks for coming on such short notice. I am eager to have my place looking better. To tell the truth, I've been feeling pretty much overwhelmed with the amount of yard work I think this place needs."

They shook hands. Luke's smile was definitely a heart stopper. She thought to herself, *What a down to earth kind of guy. Bet he is a great dad. I wonder what the story of Joel is all about?* She watched him walk back to his truck, realized she was staring, and felt her face becoming warm. What's wrong with me? Ogling a stranger's backside when Melissa's body has barely turned cold?

After Luke drove off, she finished some household chores, put the laundry away, fed the pets, took a shower and got ready for bed. Not a day went by that her thoughts didn't turn to the violent death of Melissa and nagging fears for the staff.

Her thoughts drifted over to Marino. *I know we need to have a serious talk, but I keep postponing it. I'm not ready to give up on us yet. Life could be good with Marino, but it would always have to be on his terms. If I had to worry about getting his permission or approval all the time, I couldn't stand it. I would lose a big part of myself.*

Brooksie placed a call to Lucinda and later one to Tony explaining to both the need to get together to discuss Kent and Jason as well as Melissa's memorial. They all agreed the time of the meeting to be Wednesday noon at the Table Talk Cafe. "We all need to be on the same page before Thursday's divorce group," reminded Brooksie.

CHAPTER EIGHTEEN

How poor are they that have not patience!
What wound did ever heal but by degrees?
Shakespeare, *Othello*

Wednesday noon Tony and Lucinda arrived together at the cafe. Brooksie met them at the door. They made their way to a booth near the back. Millie, one of the waitresses who had been working the cafe for many years, took their order.

"We have to make a few decisions today concerning Kent, Jason and his wife, plus what to do about clients attending the memorial service for Melissa," announced Brooksie. "I believe all of the staff are aware of the time and place already. I will email everyone just to make sure no one will be forgotten. They will have their own ideas about their clients and group members. I will also let Anita know."

"Sounds good, Brooksie. My idea is about Kent and I think we should let him have one more session before we tell him about the private investigator. Guess I'm hoping he will speak up about his past," said Lucinda.

"I agree with you Lucinda. It seems like it would be better for him if he shared the secrets in his own time," offered Tony.

"I'm okay with waiting one more week. If he doesn't come forth with information then I want to make an appointment with him, the three of us, and the investigator. We will have to pick a time that fits all five of us. Okay?" asked Brooksie.

Both nodded their heads. Next they discussed Jason and the growing concerns about his wife.

Tony remarked, "I've gotten mixed messages from Jason. At times he seemed really concerned about Loreli. At other times he shared deep negative emotions regarding his mother and women in general. I have the feeling he has harbored resentment and even hate toward his mother and dad. He has told us his dad did not do anything about the mother's infidelity."

"I sense some down deep anger he doesn't verbalize. He said he is worried about his wife, but the words don't fit his facial expressions," shared Brooksie.

"I know I'm changing the subject, but I can't seem to get something out of my mind, wakes me up at night. What did Melissa want to tell me? The message said I would be very surprised at who she had recognized at The Barn. The unnamed person was acting way out of line. If only she would have told me who it was she saw. Sorry to get us off track."

"That's okay Brooksie," offered Lucinda. "It also bothers me not knowing who she saw and could there be any connection to who she saw and her death? Let's hope your detective has some answers soon. As far as Jason goes, I agree with you both. I'm very concerned about his wife's depression, but we are only hearing his side. I would like to see for myself just how Loreli really feels.

Lucinda talked about her dread of funerals, in general. The reason given was that the ceremony became meaningless, when the speaker had not known the deceased.

"Lucinda, there is not going to be a church service. Just a gathering at Marshall's Funeral Home. Melissa is being be cremated. Her ashes are being taken by Shaun, her boyfriend. Shaun made the arrangements. Detective Marino told me the clinic lawyer, Joel Bench, had been retained by Melissa two years ago so he will be taking care of her affairs."

"That's a relief," stated Lucinda. "I think it would be just fine to let the divorce group members know when and where the memorial service is to be and leave it up to them if they want to attend or not."

Both Brooksie and Tony agreed with Lucinda.

CHAPTER NINETEEN

It is not love that is blind, but jealously.

Lawrence Durrell - *Justine*

Session Five

Jason and Kent arrived at the same time and sat next to each other. The others soon strolled in and meandered over to their chosen chairs. Tony offered a warm hello to each member and sat next to Ruth. Brooksie and Lucinda felt the need to keep up appearances; though Melissa's murder was not far from their thoughts as they greeted the members with smiles. All three facilitators had multiple thoughts buzzing through their heads. *Is it possible that Kent or Jason could be a time bomb? Is Kent's wife or Jason's wife in danger? My imagination is running wild. I used to be such a calm, balanced kind of person. Maybe Marino is right. My job is becoming more police-work oriented. I like being a cheerleader and part of someone's temporary leaning tree. I've never been a suspicious kind of person, but I'm becoming one.* Brooksie thought.

Brooksie began the session, "I will begin by saying the police have given us no more information about Melissa's death. We will share information with you soon as we have something to share. Let's begin this session by inviting anyone who wants to share this past week's happenings."

Shannon said, "I'm so sorry to hear Melissa's death was of a violent nature." She paused for a long moment then asked if she should tell about her past week.

"Absolutely Shannon." said Brooksie. "Each of you needs to remain focused on your individual tasks at hand. The next two hours are for you to concentrate on why you are in this group, what your goals and expectations for yourselves are.

"Tony, Lucinda and I are saddened by Melissa's terrible death. I believe I speak for the staff when I say none of us were close friends of Melissa, but were co-workers for several years and that has made us a sort of family. Our energy and focus is with you and this group. Shannon, please continue."

Shannon answered with an enthusiastic response, "I have some wonderful news. My son is coming home in about three weeks for a visit. I plan to give him the opportunity to tell me his thoughts and feelings about the divorce of his parents. I want to encourage him to share whatever he wants. Hopefully, I will make him comfortable enough that he will be able to talk about his feelings and not worry about mine. I want to be able to let him know I won't break, I won't be sad or mad if words come from his heart.

"I'm truly glad I'm in this group. Every time a session ends I feel like I've done a little more house cleaning. My rooms have been filled with regrets, resentments and hurts. Slowly, but surely, I'll be starting out all fresh and empty, but ready to start collecting new memories."

"I'm so glad you are going to have some time with your son. Sounds like you are developing insights as to your intrinsic worth," said Lucinda.

"Kent, I wonder if you would feel comfortable elaborating on your remark made in our last session," asked Brooksie. "I'm referring to your remarks about shame and children not being responsible for their parents mistakes, Having to pay the price for what their parents had done."

"I don't mind giving a brief summary. In fact, I want to and need to unload.

Kent cleared his throat and fidgeted in his chair. "I'm nervous. I have avoided talking about my parents my entire life, but here goes. My Dad was a criminal. He was sent to prison years ago and may still be incarcerated for all I know. He was the boss of a financial corporation. He took advantage of countless innocent and trusting customers. He robbed strangers, friends, and even a few relatives of everything they had entrusted to him. When he was in the public's eye everyone commented on what a great guy he was, but at home he was a tyrant. Mom's family, neighbors and so-called friends distanced themselves from us when dad was arrested. Mom didn't have the guts to leave him, even after he was arrested. My anger at her reached a peak when we were left penniless and she would beg, borrow or steal enough money to take the bus to visit him. She visited him faithfully. She would spend the only money we had on a damn bus ticket to see the bastard. I left home when I was seventeen and I've never looked back.

"I must sound pretty cold and heartless, but I had to save myself. Needless to say, I feel like I have been paying a huge price for my parents' behaviors. Now maybe you understand why the first word that I wrote down was shame. Shame of my parents, following a close second comes my sense of not being good enough. I don't want to become anything like my folks. I've never told Marlene about my past. I'm ashamed and embarrassed and know she would have never given me a second glance if she had known what a shitty family I hail from. I have made many poor decisions in my life. The best decision I have ever made was to love and marry Marlene."

The room is so quiet a person could hear their own heartbeat. Shannon wiped wetness from under her eyes and passed the box of Kleenix to Ruth. Ruth blew her nose with authority and blotted the tears from her cheeks.

Brooksie broke the silence. "I'm so sorry you were exposed to such cruelty as a child. You had no way to process your parents' behaviors, nor defend yourself from their disgrace.

"You have brought up a situation that to some degree is shared by others in this room as well. If things go terribly wrong in a family, it is most often the children who are quick to believe they are somehow to blame. At times they are told directly they are at fault, or less directly, by sarcasm. This lie can have a destructive ripple effect throughout their life. This childhood abuse can become a motivator for positive or negative behavior in adulthood. The choice to abuse or not to abuse will often need to be made many times in one's lifetime.

"Like Shannon, who is house cleaning and throwing out some old beliefs and myths and replacing them with honest and constructive ones. The good news is we are free to make our own good or bad choices. There is no one to blame. Our knee jerk reactions may always be close to the surface, but we get to choose how we are going to react. Easier said than done I know, because habits are tough to break."

Gage shared, "Kent, you have really given me something to chew on. I've let my parent's disgusting and hurtful marriage color my thinking to such an extent that my marriage is now possibly over. I have a different perspective now, thanks to you. My marriage was about two people, not four."

Lucinda asked Cecelia, "Are you gaining anything from the conversation about children and parents?"

"Absolutely. "I'm learning to be more understanding, more compassionate with others including myself. So I made a mistake.

I chose poorly, but I experienced great joy for a short time. Loving someone is a gift we give away. If the gift is not appreciated, returned, unopened or thrown away, the receiver is the loser not the other way around. At the end of the day, Raul is the loser."

"I'm working on helping my kids express their feelings. I want to make sure they understand they are not in any way to blame for the misery caused by me or their dad or any other adults in their lives," said Melika.

Ruth blew her nose noisily again, then straightened her dress for the umpteenth time and said, "I don't know how to feel or what to say right at this moment. I didn't measure up to my brother in my parents eyes. That is a fact. I'm not smart, clever or pretty and that too is a fact. My children have been my life and now this group makes me feel guilty about my treatment of my ex-husband and my kids. What am I supposed to do? I need someone or something to blame for my miserable life. I didn't ask to be born stupid, slow and ugly."

Tony faced Ruth and spoke in a soft voice with noticeable gentle overtones. "Ruth do you consider yourself a good cook?"

"I'm not what you call an expert. You don't see me on the television cooking shows. I don't cook fancy like, but I have cooked decent, tasty, rib-filling meals. I've cooked and baked a truck load of good eating for many years. Actually I've had lots of women from my church compliment my pies and cakes. Many have asked for my recipes. Fact is I never use a recipe I just know what goes with what, never measure and somehow most everything comes out pretty good."

"Ruth, I bet you have had a sick husband and kids and even some injuries happened to your family, over the years, true?" asked Tony.

"I've done my share of nursing duties. We never have enough money for all our needs. So over the years, I've learned how to come up with my own cures or whatever is needed. I didn't fix broken bones or stuff like that, but I was real cool in an emergency. I even saved one of my sons when he was five or six. He had swallowed a grape and couldn't breathe. I just knew what I had to do and I did it."

"Seems to me," said Tony, "You have some important skills and talents. Homemaking is a vital career for a successful family unit. Sounds like you have done many of your homemaking jobs very well. If you think about your experiences as a parent more, I believe you will discover more of your strengths and focus less on what you consider your flaws."

"A good point, Tony," responded Brooksie. "Ruminating about our so-called flaws is a waste of time. I've been working on that lesson myself. Ruth, I hope you will pat yourself on the back for all of the 'jobs' you have done well even without the help of education or high grades. You are self-taught and that is something to be truly be proud of. You would have been a fine pioneer woman because you can make do with whatever you have. A true-blue survivor."

Jason looked around and his eyes rested on Lucinda. "It is true, beauty is only skin deep. What lies beneath cannot be hidden by a gorgeous frame. My mother was drop dead beautiful on the outside and soul-ugly on the inside.

"I'm going to continue to encourage Lorelie to go to counseling. Maybe I'll take her shopping, that used to cheer her up. It's hard for me to see her looking so unhappy."

Debriefing

Lucinda spoke first. Her eyes sparkled and her hands waved all around her. "I was so excited to hear Kent open up and now I feel he should be aware of what the investigator has uncovered. I also think his wife should be present. What do you guys think?"

"I agree," said Brooksie. "I'll call and make an appointment with him and Mr. Edwards. How about Monday 11 a.m. for you two?'

They both said that time was okay if she could get Kent and Mr. Edwards also. Brooksie felt it would be a mistake ethically to invite the wife. "After Kent hears the report he can invite her for a later time. Confidentiality can be tricky."

Tony stated his daughter would be in school so that time was fine with him.

"So we agree to the time. I might as well place the call right now to Mr. Edwards and if he is available I will call Kent."

She dialed Mr. Edward's office and got an okay from the secretary for Monday. After a few deep breaths, she dialed Kent's number. He answered on the second ring. Brooksie asked if he could come to the office on Monday at 11 a.m. for a private session with Lucinda, Tony and herself.

"Am I in trouble? I was afraid I had said too much,"said Kent.

"No, Kent, you are definitely not in trouble. We simply want to share some information with you that has come to our attention. I think you will benefit by the new knowledge. The fact is, your sister-law apparently hired a private investigator to do a background check on you. The investigator found some information about your past that your sister-in law told to your wife. The investigator has agreed to meet with you and us to share his findings. Can you make it to the office Monday at 11 a.m.?"

There was a long silent pause at the other end of the phone and Brooksie wondered if Kent was still on the line.

"I'll be there. I can't believe Rayana was so jealous of me. She must really hate me and now I have lost Marlene forever. She will never trust me again. What if Marlene comes to the meeting and hears for herself what really happened years back? Would one of you be willing to invite Marlene? I'm afraid she wouldn't show if I made the request."

Brooksie agreed to invite Marlene, but told Kent he needed to reassure the staff that Marlene would be completely safe if she came to the office.

Kent hesitated briefly, his voice quivered and he said, "I've never physically harmed any woman. I did not hurt or kill my first wife. I've been seriously mad at two women in my life, my Mom and Marlene's sister, yet I have never had thoughts to physically harm either one of them. I might have wished them an early natural death, but nothing else."

"Okay. I'll call her. What's her number? She's going to ask me what you have to do with the Grief Clinic. Do I have your permission to tell her you have been attending a divorce support group and will you sign a permission slip Monday morning?"

"Yes, say what you need to. I trust your judgment. If she won't come will we still meet with the investigator? By the way her number is 260-4440."

"Thanks for the number and yes to your question. See you Monday at 11 a.m."

Brooksie looked at the other two and gave a thumbs up. "Now let's finish our debriefing. I saw Gage reacting to Kent's sharing. He seems to be listening with both heart and ears to the others. Tony, you were certainly on the mark with Ruth. You are a natural at this kind of support work. Parents' cruelty to their offspring or actually any abuse to the young never ceases to make me heart sick.

"You pointed out her strengths and I doubt that has ever been done for Ruth."

"I would like to lock up her parents and my mother in the same house for a year or two. Maybe they would start to recognize their own meanness. Miracles do happen and even the nastiest people can have a change of heart, but I'm not going to hold my breath waiting for any changes in my mother's behavior," said Lucinda.

"I've got to admit that five weeks ago I wasn't sure I would ever feel kindly towards Ruth, but today I feel quite different. So is the change with Ruth or with me?" asked Tony.

"I'd say both of you are softening, because for the first time, Ruth is experiencing some acceptance and appreciation. Some from you and the group which in turn is helping her to feel better about herself. A window has opened ever so slightly to give her a glimpse of just how cruel her parents treated her," added Brooksie.

"Her religious beliefs are deeply embedded in her. The commandments to honor her parents has been thrown at her for years. How do you reconcile your chosen dogma when your parents don't deserve to be honored? She's had to swallow her pain, resentment and questions because the church sets the rules. It seems she has been torn between denial of her feelings about parental abuse and her unquestioning beliefs in the church's teachings."

"Facilitating groups is an eye opening experience, an honor and definitely a form of higher education. I love this work," shared Lucinda.

"I say, ditto. I'm beginning to understand why you both love your jobs," added Tony.

"Well, if we are done, at Kent's request, I'm going to place a call to his wife, to invite her to the meeting. I don't like having to do this."

Brooksie dialed the number given to her by Kent. A woman answered and Brooksie asked to speak to Marlene.

"This is Marlene."

Brooksie told her about the meeting for Monday with Kent, the staff and the private investigator. Marlene was soft-spoken and she asked a few questions which Brooksie said would be better answered in the meeting. Kent's wife said she would show up at the appointed time and then asked if she should bring her sister. Brooksie said probably not unless she first spoke with Kent to get his okay. She also told her the investigator would want to get in touch with her sister at a later date.

Brooksie took a deep breath after hanging up. She noticed her hands were shaky and slightly moist. *Somehow I know Marino would not approve of what I'm doing. What's wrong with this picture? I'm not a kid. I don't need to get approval to do what I think is right. Damn you Marino.*

CHAPTER TWENTY

**Fate makes our relatives,
choice makes our friends.**
Jacques Delille - *Malheur et pitie*

As soon as Brooksie arrived home after work, she checked on each member of her furry companions. She also counted to make sure Aunt Tilly hadn't made an unannounced visit.

Next she checked for phone messages and received a surprise. She had a call from Rafael, Marino's sister.

She dialed Rafael's number and her call was answered before the second ring.

"Hello Brooksie. Thanks for returning my call."

"I'm glad to hear from you, Rafael. Is everything okay?"

"Yes. I just wanted to know if you have time to go to lunch tomorrow? I'll be in town for a short time. I have to return home again in the afternoon," answered Rafael.

"I would love to meet with you. Where would you like to have lunch?" asked Brooksie.

"I'm not familiar enough with your area to choose any place. Could you pick a restaurant for us?"

"Sure," responded Brooksie. "The Table Talk Cafe is near my office and I can be there at 12:15."

"I know that cafe. Blake has taken me there a few times. I'll be there at 12:15. See you tomorrow. Thanks for agreeing to meet me on such short notice," answered Rafael.

Next day both women arrived at the café at the same time. They shared an enthusiastic embrace and walked inside. Brooksie spotted a small table by the window and they made their way over to it. They both ordered salads. Brooksie waited quietly for Rafael to begin the conversation. Rafael clasped and unclasped her fingers numerous times. She took the napkin off of the table, placed it on her lap and then put it back in its original position on the table.

"Guess I surprised you by calling and asking you to meet me today?"

"A surprise yes, but a very pleasant one."

Rafael continued, "You asked about my Dad and I wanted tell you more about him and Blake, but I needed privacy. Dad was difficult, more like impossible. Mom, Blake, and I had to be careful around him. His coworkers thought of him as quite the gentleman, but at home he was a tyrant. He was hardest on Blake and Mom. He slapped my mother a few times that I knew about. I could often hear him berate, saying mean things to her. There were a few times bruises appeared on her face. She would try to cover them with makeup, but I knew what she was doing. I hated that she put up with such demeaning treatment. One time he shoved her so hard she fell over the kitchen chair and broke her arm. I saw that with my own eyes. I was coming home early and neither of them knew I was there. They never knew that I had actually seen Dad push Mom. Guess I was afraid to confront either one of them. Mom always made excuses for Dad, claiming he had a difficult and dangerous job and was under a great deal of stress.

"If Blake made our father mad, he would get hit with a belt. Blake never cried, but he often couldn't sit down for a day or two after a beating.

"I heard Dad say many times, 'A woman's place is in the home raising their children. The man is in charge because that's how it's always been.'

"I think my brother feared and admired our father at the same time.

"To this day mom refuses to say one negative word about Dad. Drives me crazy because I know he constantly made her feel bad, stupid, unattractive and inefficient. He would say, 'Aren't you putting on a little weight Marcella? I think I see a few grey hairs. Aging isn't going to be kind to you my dear. You know I can fit in the same size as I did in my early twenties.'

"If Mom made any sort of complaint or request, Dad would shout her down. He kept all of us on a short leash and a strict budget.

"Blake would kill me if he knew I told you any of this."

Rafael stopped long enough to chew on a fingernail and then continued, "One day my brother and I were downtown to see a movie. Across the street from the theater was a famous restaurant. We both were stunned speechless at seeing our righteous father walking into that lavish restaurant with a beautiful woman expensively dressed. They were holding hands.

"I wanted to run into the restaurant and confront the lying tyrant, but Blake became furious with me and told me we were never to say anything to Dad or Mom about what we had seen.

"A few months before dad was killed, we had a fight. I wanted to go out with a friend from school. Dad forbade me from dating him, saying Wade was bad news. He told me Wade came from a mixed background and 'that kind always makes trouble.'

"That really made me angry and I blurted out, 'you're a damn hypocrite. Blake and I both saw you last week walking into a fancy restaurant with some expensively dressed woman and you were holding hands.' In my heart of hearts I wish my Mom heard us, but if she did, she never let on.

"He remained silent and the all the color drained from his face. I told him I was going out with Wade and for him to never again tell me what I could or could not do. He was killed a few weeks later. He died a hero, but he wasn't my hero, alive or dead.

"Mom and Blake continue to remember him and talk about him as if he was such a great husband and father."

Brooksie placed her hand gently over Rafael's hand. "I'm sorry your father's death came so soon after your argument. Maybe it was a good thing you finally stood up for yourself. Are you feeling guilty about the argument?"

"I used to, but no more. I'm glad I called him a hypocrite. I feel bad that we never told our mother about his secret life. Maybe the facts could have helped her to bring him down off of the pedestal. She could possibly have had a happier, and more honest life with or without him. He purposely worked at destroying her self-respect. In my book, he was a bully."

Brooksie responded, "Rafael I will not repeat anything you have told me about your dad, but I would like to ask you a question. Do you have any idea why your brother would be set against adopting kids?"

"I'm not sure what Blake thinks or feels, but I do remember Dad talking about the importance of family genes. 'Family is everything and that means stay with your own kind.' Dad had dealings with foster kids and blamed their heredity for their criminal behaviors.

"Do you think you two will get married? Sorry, I know it's none of my business, but I am curious," asked Rafael.

"I don't mind you asking. I don't know the answer. Your brother and I have some very different ideas on a few important issues. Some having to do with my work and the other having to do with children. I do love him, but I can't ignore the red flags. We may not be good for each other in the long run. I would never be happy if someone was trying to dominate my career and would want only his own biological children. His need and desire to be the decision maker would possibly escalate and infringe on other matters in the future. I would never be happy with a dictator for a mate. I want a partner, not a boss.

"What's important to you Rafael in a partner?"

Rafael answered, "I definitely want children. If for some reason we couldn't have any, I would adopt or maybe even foster. I want someone who shows affection, is generous with money and time, and has a good job he likes. He must like children and be happy. I enjoy my family and friends. I would like my Mom and brother to like him, but if they didn't it wouldn't be a deal breaker."

"Are you seeing anyone special?" asked Brooksie.

"Sort of. Blake doesn't know about him and Mom has met him only once. He's a fireman. He's thirty, married once when he was twenty years old. The marriage lasted less than a year, no kids involved. He is lots of fun, doesn't push the sex thing, but he is a great kisser. I just like being with him. I feel I can be myself when I'm with him. I don't ever have to walk on egg shells and worry if I'm going to upset him."

"Rafael, I hope you take enough time to get to know him, at least to know how he feels about the things that are important to you and vice versa."

"Thanks Brooksie for listening and for being so open with me. Mom and Blake are pretty closed mouthed. I know one thing for certain, I don't want a marriage like Mom's. I'd rather join a convent than become some guy's house maid."

"I'm glad we met today, Rafael. No matter what happens between your brother and me, please consider me a friend. I would welcome your calls or visits anytime."

CHAPTER TWENTY-ONE

**No one can make you feel inferior
without your consent.**
Eleanor Roosevelt - *This Is My Story*

Session Six

Cecelia and Kent entered the group room together. They stood close to one another and appeared to be in deep conversation. They sat down in chairs next to each other.

Shannon, Melika, and Ruth arrived at the door simultaneously followed shortly by Gage.

Gage was grinning from ear to ear. Shannon also looked like she just won the lottery. She was dressed in bright shades of red and had obviously made an attempt to fix her hair in a different style, almost becoming.

Jason arrived late and beads of perspiration showed on his forehead. "I was afraid to leave Loreli this evening. She looked so lost this morning. I asked Mrs. Long, a neighbor who lives next door on our right, to check on her in one hour. She said she will knock on our door an hour after I've left and pretend to need to borrow something, like sugar or whatever. Loreli would be furious if she knew I had asked Mrs. Long to check on her."

"Is your wife still refusing to see a counselor?" asked Tony.

"Yes. I've talked myself blue in the face about her needing professional help. I haven't given up and will try again this coming week. It has become increasingly difficult for me to be comfortable about going to my office," he sighed. "Well, enough about my problems, let's get on with the group business."

Brooksie began, "Today we ask you to focus on a specific subject. The first topic is about what you feel you have done right in your marriage and then what you wish you would have done differently.

"Secondly, please address how your divorce or separation is affecting your kids, if you have kids.

"Thirdly, how have you been affected by your own parent's divorce or by their lifestyle? We will give you a few minutes to write down whatever comes to mind about the questions I've just listed."

Tony passed around tablets and pencils. Some immediately began to jot down words while others stared off into space. Ruth and Jason are the last to put pencil to paper.

Cecelia is the first one to finish writing. A few minutes pass and Lucinda asked for volunteers to share whatever they had written.

Cecelia looked at her notes and said, "I don't think I've made many mistakes during my marriage. My giant mistake was made before we said the vows. I didn't take enough time pre-marriage to get a better understanding of Raul's character. I was afraid if I waited he would lose interest.

"Desperation, lack of belief in my own desirability and value were my pre-marriage mistakes. I believe I was good wife. I treated Raul the way I wanted to be treated and I'd do it again, if I'm ever in a romantic relationship.   "In my opinion, my parents did a fine job of raising me. They encouraged and insisted I do my best in school. They were both professionals and older than the parents of my friends. I grew up around adults. My parents were quite formal, always dressed nicely, never in Levis or tennis shoes. They were knick-named Mr. Stuffy and Mrs. Prim by my two closest friends. Life was a serious matter to them. They were kind and we were a happy, but very conservative, somewhat formal, and definitely a serious family.

"Raul did teach me how to lighten up and just have fun for fun's sake. I give credit to him for teaching me to be more spontaneous and even silly once in a while."

Kent spoke up next. "I know now that keeping secrets about my past from Marlene was wrong. Secrets can be used against a person. I love her and always did whatever I thought pleased her, made her smile. Making her happy was my every day goal. Obviously, keeping my past from her was a mistake. I felt like I was fighting the wind, before I found out what my sister-in-law had told Marlene. Now I may have a chance to set it right.

"I've already told all of you about my parents and how difficult it was for me growing up. I've kept many secrets, fearing negative judgments by others. Guess that makes me a coward. I've heard that confession is good for the soul, but laying it all out there is risky business. Innocent until proven guilty is not the way I have found the world to work."

Kent begins to doodle on the tablet and to squirm in his chair. He picks an imaginary hair or whatever off his shirt sleeve and continues to doodle.

Jason focusing his eyes on Kent's face, said, "I understand exactly what you are talking about. I kept my parent's relationship with me and with each other a secret. I was confused, ashamed and mortified all at the same time. People can be cruel when they make rash judgments, with little information."

Ruth nodded. She is wearing a most homely outfit, her hair looks like it was arranged by a bird hurrying to throw a nest together. She has on no make-up and her fingernails are in desperate need of a manicure. She was the perfect contestant or applicant for a complete make-over show.

With a hostile expression towards Kent she said, "You could be wearing ragged, dirty and ugly clothes and you would still look like a handsome model. I could be dressed in a queen's wardrobe and I would still look like something the cat dragged in, but we do have something in common. We both have parents who hurt us by making us embarrassed to be ourselves. Like maybe we weren't worthy of anything really good. Don't get me wrong, I'm not comparing you and me, just the message we grew up believing.

"You're absolutely right, Ruth," responded Kent. "I think I have always been afraid the world would find out I have nothing to offer, I'm a phony, make-believe human, a scared little boy afraid of the people finding out I am hollow inside."

Lucinda wiped away small trails of mascara slowly making their way down her checks. "I can totally relate to you both. My mother has verbally beaten me up since I was a little girl. She was jealous of my relationship with dad. After dad left us. she blamed me for everything she considered bad, unpleasant and unwanted in her life. It has taken me many years to realize I've never been to blame for her miserable existence, her depression, loneliness and other miseries. I actually believed all or part of her rotten life was somehow my fault. Because of this belief and guilt I choose my relationships very poorly. They only reinforced what I already believed about myself; I wasn't worth keeping around. Deep down I didn't believe I deserved to be happy. I was the bad seed and needed to be punished and shunned. It is true we attract people who will confirm our worst fears about ourselves.

"I stayed too long with partners who didn't like themselves either. They treated me with disrespect, cruelty and deceit. I married two times and both times I made the same mistakes. My own ego got in the way of reality so I pretended I was saving their lives, like I had superpowers.

"My Dad did the same thing. He allowed my mother to manipulate him and I did the same stupid thing with my husbands. I have been a coward and a phony too, Kent. I followed in my father's footsteps. We both thought we could change another person's thoughts and behaviors. We didn't accept responsibility for our own happiness and made excuses for our unwillingness to improve our own personal situation."

"The mistake I've made in my married life has to do with trusting," said Jason. "My mother's constant unfaithfulness, my Dad's addiction to working every moment, his trusting Mom, and his eventual denial of her philandering was a powerful lesson for me. That is why I'm so shocked by the way Loreli has changed. I believed I had finally found a completely trustworthy woman. I must have been blind. I still am. I missed all the signs of her unhappiness. Maybe I've turned into my Dad after all. What a frightening thought that is."

Brooksie asked, "Jason you have been speaking about what you feel you did wrong. What did you do that was right?"

"We took some wonderful trips, shopping sprees for her, treated her like a queen. I believed I was taking care of her every need. I complimented her for something every day. I don't know what else I should have done," replied Jason.

Tony spoke to Jason, "I also felt I was doing everything possible to make my wife content, but what I didn't understand for a long time was that my wife was suffering with a mental illness. I thought she was depressed about something particular and she would get over it. Fact is she was clinically depressed and unable to find her way back to reality and joy.

"My mistake was thinking I was doing something that was the cause of her depression instead of realizing her body's chemicals were working against us. I was slow in finding proper medical care for her.

"The thing I did right was finding medical assistance and keeping our baby girl safe from her mentally ill mother.

"It wasn't my divorce that negatively affected my daughter. It was her mother's illness, the erratic behaviors and the pendulum swinging of her mother's moods.

"My parents didn't divorce, but I believe my life and theirs would have been better if they'd gone their separate ways. The silence of unspoken resentment can often be ear shattering, almost deafening. My mother was relentlessly demanding and complaining. In my opinion, my father was a coward."

"I guess it's my turn," said Gage. "In the beginning of our marriage I was more interested in what my wife needed and wanted. The honeymoon lasted for many years. So what I did right was to listen to her and really try hard to hear what she was telling me.

"What I did wrong was, I stopped listening and I focused totally on my needs and that of the family in general. My only goal was to bring home the bacon, forgetting individual needs. I've already talked about my parent's parallel marriage and how empty that felt. I always knew I didn't want that kind of a marriage. I wanted to do things as a family. I think I simply forget that a good marriage doesn't mean we had to do everything together. We didn't always have to be on the same page. We needed separation of some activities just to keep ourselves interesting to our partner."

Melika's turn came and she said in her soft voice, "I did marry for love, but also to get away from my toxic home. I had lots of feelings for my husband in the beginning. I enjoyed being a wife, keeping house and having precious babies. Looking back, I think my main motivation for getting married so young was to get away from my mother's domination and unkindness.

"I wish I would've taken off the blinders when I constantly observed my parents and their sick relationship. Maybe I would have figured out my own relationship was turning into the same horrible drama as my folks. I wish I would've been wiser, stronger and braver than my father."

"I picked the wrong partner, but I don't believe that was my fault. What I did wrong was to stay with the wrong person for so long," said Shannon.

"What I did right was to have loved my son unconditionally and to have taught him from infancy that he was valued and cherished. And failing at something didn't mean he was a failure, but continuing to try would make him a success.'

"I wish, like you Melika, I had been more assertive, wiser and more courageous. I can't look back anymore and keep wishing it was different. I'm going to focus on today and how to treat myself with far more respect and give myself pats on the back when I feel I deserve them."

"Shannon, I totally agree that we can become our own heroes," offered Brooksie. "I've never been married so I have no first-hand experience about what works and what doesn't. I do think it is important that couples agree on big issues before they commit to each other. The big ones like children, finances, religion and others. I'm always learning from the members of every group I've been in. I'm definitely becoming wiser about relationships just by listening to all of you. I feel fortunate to have so many fine teachers.

"Our time is over for this evening. We want to invite you to the memorial for Melissa. One of us will call you or send an email and give you the time, date and place where it will be held. Please don't feel obligated to come, but if you choose to come you will be welcomed. I will tell you so far there has been no further information from the police as to the perpetrator's identity. Goodnight and please drive safely."

Debriefing

"I'm concerned about Jason and his wife. If what he tells us about her, is true, she might very well be clinically depressed. I'm thinking of calling him and asking him point blank if he thinks she might be suicidal. If he says yes, I'm going to recommend he insist she see a doctor or therapist. I will go over the signs of impending suicide so at least he may be armed with the warning signs."

"I feel the same way," commented Lucinda. "I would remind him about "well checks" the police will do if he becomes anymore concerned when he is away from her. I know he mentioned his wife freaking out if she was being checked on, but better safe than sorry."

"Good suggestion," responded Brooksie.

"You two are way out of my league. So whatever you think is best," said Tony.

"A lot of great insights were shared by all of the group members tonight. It never ceases to amaze me how people can share a similar problem and can be so helpful to each other to find their own answers or solutions for themselves.

"I'm ready to call it a night. I'm really worn out, mostly emotionally. How about you two?"

Both nodded. They locked up and went to their cars. Tony again waited for both women to drive off before he left the parking lot.

CHAPTER TWENTY-TWO

**Oh, what a tangled web we weave
When first we practice to deceive.**
Sir Walter Scott - *Marmion*

Brooksie received a call from someone she would have never expected to hear from. Melissa's temporary replacement, Janice. She informed Brooksie of a call from Mrs. Woods. "She said she is the wife of Jason who is attending one of our groups. You told me to refer all calls to you unless they ask for someone by name."

"Thanks Janice. I'll take the call. Thanks also for taking over on such short notice and in such difficult circumstances."

Brooksie hesitated before picking up the receiver. *My God this divorce group is getting complicated. Any more intrigue and maybe I should consider opening my own detective agency. Marino would hate what's going on right now. Better I don't tell him.*

"Hello, this is Brooksie Everett. How can I help you, Mrs. Woods?"

"I don't know exactly what you can do for me. I need to talk with someone about my husband Jason. I know he goes to your clinic every Thursday night. I'm not sure what he's doing there.

"I'm not sure if I should be talking to you, but I do have some serious concerns about him," continued Loreli Woods.

Brooksie responded, "Confidentiality for all clients is the rule. I cannot say yes or no if your husband is attending the clinic. I hope you understand."

"I do understand. All I ask is to meet with someone from the clinic so that I can share my concerns. I won't expect you to give me any answers. Please, I need to talk to someone," pleaded Loreli.

Brooksie took several deep breaths and thought, *This is the second person in only a few weeks who wants to discuss a client in the divorce group. I don't like it. Feels like cloak and dagger stuff.* "I can meet you at the public library one hour from now. It's only a few blocks from the clinic. Do you know where it is?"

"Yes I do. Thanks for agreeing to meet with me. I'll be in a bright pink outfit and I'll wait by the front entrance. See you in an hour," answered Loreli.

Those bright colors don't match with someone depressed. "See you in one hour by the entrance Mrs. Woods."

One hour later, Brooksie was standing in front of the library and she spotted a strikingly attractive woman in a hot pink outfit. They introduced themselves, entered the library, and quickly found a private corner with two chairs. Loreli Woods looked even more stunning than Jason described in group, thought Brooksie. Loreli looked around the room nervously and played with her beautifully manicured nails. She told Brooksie Jason had been acting strangely for many months.

"I know you said you can't verify his attending a group. But several weeks back, maybe it was more like five or six weeks, I found a receipt he'd paid the clinic. It was attached to a pamphlet and Divorce Group was circled as was your name. I'll just tell you all I can about my concerns, or better said my fears. You don't have to say anything.

"Our first two years or so were great, but Jason has become more and more controlling. He didn't even want me to see friends or talk on the phone with them.

"He became very upset with I talked about wanting to get pregnant and even accused me of trying to trick him by stopping my birth control pills. He yelled at me, 'You are just like the others.'

"I asked him what others? When we were dating he told me he was a bachelor. He said he never had wanted to get married before he met me. The more questions I asked, the madder he became and stormed out of the house and didn't return for hours. When he eventually came home he acted like everything was okay. He told me we could talk about having kids later. He said our anniversary was only six months away and we would see what we wanted to do then. I have no idea what he meant, but it sent chills down my spine.

"He has changed. He doesn't talk to me anymore. I'm embarrassed to say this, but now he wants rough sex when he wants me at all. Maybe it is just the middle age thing. I'm at a loss and frightened at the same time. Sometimes he seems to be really depressed. I've never in my life had that sort of problem. I'm confused about what is wrong with Jason. All my life I've been the half-full glass kind of person. Jason used to tell me he loved my happy-go-lucky personality. I don't know who to turn to. I don't have any real family and only one girlfriend. She is worried about me and tells me to just leave him. I'm not sure what he would do if I tried to."

Brooksie hesitated momentarily before making suggestions. She felt totally confused and even blindsided seeing Jason's wife looking the opposite of Jason's portrayal of her. She glanced around the room as if looking for answers. The movie star appearance of the woman sitting in front of her wasn't at all like Jason's description.

"I'm going to give you some information you may find helpful. First, please take this name and number down."

Loreli took out a small notebook and pen and waited.

Brooksie continued, "This is the number for Detective Blake Marino. He works for the Whitefall Police Department. You might want to call him, make an appointment with him and talk over your concerns. He can direct you to the best person to see.

"Secondly, counseling is another possibility. It can be as a couple or individually."

"Jason has already angrily refused counseling. Last week I asked him why he was so mad at me. He just stared at me for a long time and said, he wasn't mad just disappointed and all good things have to end. He said everything will work out and for me to just be patient. Maybe he is gathering information from your group as to the best way to get rid of me by divorcing me."

"Loreli, as I told you on the phone I cannot say if your husband is attending a group at the clinic. I can strongly urge you to listen to your gut feelings. If you feel you are in danger, then go to the police. You have Detective Marino's name and I can give you the name of a psychologist whose specialty is working with abused women, if you want. There are also shelters available for emergencies, including going directly to the police station, fire station and most any public place if you believe you are in any immediate danger."

"Ms. Everett, I'm grateful for your suggestions. I do have one other serious concern and it is about Jason himself. I'm going to tell you this just in case he is in one of your groups. I think he may be thinking about hurting himself. When he gets real quiet and isolates himself in our den I worry what he might be doing. He goes to work every day, but he is not the same person I married. I am afraid of him, but I'm also afraid for him."

Loreli said she would call the detective and the psychologist and make appointments with both. She also said she would ask Marcia, a friend, for the name of a lawyer. She thanked Brooksie for listening and they went their separate ways.

Brooksie remained on the library steps for a few minutes watching Loreli drive off in her fancy car. *Something just didn't feel right about Loreli's story. One of them is not telling the truth, but why and which one is lying? Could be some serious mental problems, even illness be involved? I better call Marino right away and let him know she might call him.*

As soon as Brooksie arrived at the clinic, she made a beeline to the phone in her office and called Mr. Bench, the clinic's attorney followed by a call to the detective.

CHAPTER TWENTY-THREE

**Experience is a hard teacher because she
gives the test first, the lessons afterwards.**
Vernon Law - *This Week*

Kent, Marlene and Mr. Edwards arrived within minutes of each other at the Grief Clinic office. Brooksie took care of the introductions and all followed her into one of the comfortable rooms used for groups. She closed the door and took a seat. The others followed suit.

Tony sat between Mr. Edwards and Kent. Lucinda and Brooksie both sat opposite Kent and Marlene purposely to observe their body language.

Mr. Edwards opened his briefcase and pulled out a folder.

"Kent, I was hired by your sister-in-law to gather the information in this file. I notified Miss Everett of my findings out of concern for your wife's safety."

"What the hell are you talking about? My wife's safety? You think she is in danger from me? She is the only good thing in my life. I would take a bullet for her without a second thought!"

Kent gave Marlene a questioning look. "Are you really afraid of me?"

Before she had a chance to respond, Mr. Edwards spoke up. "Please let me finish before you start asking questions of your wife. I want you to look over this file. If you have any questions or comments I'll be happy to answer them if I can."

He handed the folder to Kent, who yanked the folder away, nostrils flaring. Kent seemed on the brink of losing his temper. His breathing was noticeably louder. Ten minutes passed as Kent, with wrinkled brow, read the six pages from the file. The minutes moved by slower than an old snail. Time seemed to stand still to the three facilitators. Not one of them took their eyes off of Kent or Marlene.

Kent finally looked up. He addressed Brooksie. "For the most part, all of the information is correct. I did change my last name because it would have given away my heritage. I've told the support group about my shame over having a criminal for a father and a worthless mother. All of my other relatives, friends and neighbors shunned Mom and me. I was just a kid and was being treated like the bad seed.

"This report makes my first wife's death sound suspicious. I assume that is why safety of Marlene is an issue. I'll tell you who the dangerous one is, my vicious sister-in-law.

"I'm sorry Marlene, I never told you about my Dad or my first wife. I was too afraid you wouldn't want anything to do with me if you knew about my disgusting past."

Marlene, with her head bowed and her hands clasped in her lap said in a whisper, "I wish you could have trusted me, Kent. I'm not a judgmental kind of person."

"I, too, wish I had trusted you," answered Kent. "I never thought your sister Rayana was so hateful and selfish to do what she did. Obviously, she would do anything to keep her generous income flowing in from you. She must see me as a threat to her financial future. She is devious, selfish and excuse my French, one lying bitch. I'm sorry to speak about her this way Marlene, but she's costing us our most wonderful marriage."

Tony asked, " Can you say more about your first wife's death?"

"Certainly," answered Kent. "Our marriage was not a love match. I was her showpiece. I'm not proud of my role, nor do I think I'm that great. I was paid well and she treated well. We had some good times together. Early on she told me about her heart condition. She informed me, before we married, about the possibility of an early death for her. Looking back, I believe she had a fatalistic attitude and she had decided to sow all the wild oats she could while she had time. I, on the other hand, was a very angry man. I was angry at the world and everyone in it. I wanted payback for the treatment I received as a kid. I was into the blame game with both feet.

"Raylene Whitfield was her name. She wanted a 'young stud' to show off to her so-called friends. We were both living shallow and phony lives. She was loaded and willing to buy a boy toy. This is hard for me to talk about because I was a jerk, an empty shell, devoid of any good traits during that time. I didn't have an education or any kind of career. I wanted to be rich. I believed money would make me feel good about myself. Love only meant getting hurt.

"Raylene didn't tell anybody about her damaged heart because she denied any imperfections. She had had scarlet fever as a kid plus some other childhood problems, I can't remember what they were right now. You can get your hands on her old medical records if you want.

"For the most part she treated me fine. We really had some good times. I believe Raylene was also an angry person. She didn't ever talk about her past except to say her parents should never have tried parenthood. She also said the only good she received from them was a boatload of money.

"Her death was sudden and painless, for which I was grateful. She had no living relatives. She left everything to me. I went pretty crazy after her death because of the huge inheritance. I was aware that her friends looked at me with disgust and some with suspicion. I just didn't give a damn. I cared less about what they or anyone thought of me. I made many stupid, poor financial decisions.

"Eventually I got my priorities straight. I was finally ready to take responsibility for my own life and quit blaming my messed-up parents for my bad decisions as an adult.

"Marlene came along and I fell in love for the first time." Kent stopped talking and gently took Marlene's hand with his. She didn't resist. "She was and is kind, fun, generous, loving, compassionate and more interested in others than in herself. I had never known anyone like her.

"She knows her sister is selfish and a leech, but Marlene loves her and wants her to be happy and secure. I know this shocks you Marlene and you will feel hurt by what Rayana has done. Basically Rayana has been trying to break us up since our second date."

Lucinda asked, "What is your next step, Kent? What do you plan to do with the information Mr. Edwards has provided?"

"I don't know. I just want to talk in private with Marlene and apologize for not telling her the truth about my past. If I had not kept secrets from her maybe none of this would have ever happened.

"I don't want her to feel she has to choose between her sister and me. I believe she loves us both." Kent turns toward Marlene and said in almost a whisper, "Hopefully you can forgive me for withholding so much from you."

Tears slowly found their way down Marlene's cheeks and Kent, ever so gently, brushed them away. His eyes were also glistening.

Both Lucinda and Brooksie were dabbing their eyes with tissues. Tony blew his nose.

The discussion continued for the next half hour. Marlene and Kent still holding hands discussed what to do about Rayana. Marlene also apologized for not simply asking Kent about the truth of the report.

Mr. Edwards stated he would be sending a letter to Rayana explaining the legality of his actions because of the possibility of harm to Marlene from her husband.

Everyone stood up and shook Mr. Edward's hand. Kent looked ecstatic and bear-hugged his wife and then grabbed both Lucinda and Brooksie and hugged them as well. Tony shook hands with Marlene and Kent and wished them well.

The last to leave were the facilitators. They in unison said, "Wow! A great ending." The three were walking on clouds as they went about their day.

CHAPTER TWENTY-FOUR

**There are two ways to run a relationship-one
is like a team, and the other is like a contest.**
Andrew Matthews - *Follow Your Heart*

Friday around 5:30 p.m., Luke Jones, the prospective
gardener/landscaper arrived at Brooksie's home. Many of the pets
gathered around Luke for the crotch greeting by the taller dogs
and the rubbing against his legs by the smaller critters. Once the
introductions were finished and Luke had petted most, he rolled
out his landscape plans on her dining table.

"This looks wonderful," said Brooksie. "My uncle was right;
you are definitely a talented landscaper. I love the stone pathways
that wander through the back yard. The patio and fire pit are
fantastic. The cats will love the jungle-like vines and bushes to
hide behind or in and the dogs have plenty of room to run and
cavort. I'm lucky the six- foot stone fence was here when I bought
the place."

"I'm glad you like my ideas. I can give you an estimate of cost
and a time frame if you want?" Looking directly into Brooksie's
dark chocolate eyes Luke said, "Your aunt tells me you like to
play tennis."

"My dear aunt is like a human Facebook. She puts it all out
there for the world to read. She is looking and always listening for

a weak spot to find an appropriate forever home for a homeless creature or a mate for me. She is relentless in her quest of matchmaking for pets or people. In a second, it seems she can spot if someone is a patsy for a pet sob story. "Yes." To your question about tennis. I'm not competition material, but I do love to play. And "yes" to wanting an estimate of price and time."

Brooksie felt her face growing warm from Luke's intense eye-to-eye contact. A barely visible smile started at the corner of his lips as he turned his attention to his plans on the table.

"Back to my precious aunt who I've seen in action many times. I was appalled once when she was able to convince a woman who was highly allergic to cat dander, to be talked into going to an allergist and start treatment for cat allergies. Even while the potential pet owner was coughing and sneezing, my sweet Aunt Tilly was handing her two cats that needed a home.

"After the lady promised to make a doctor's appointment, my aunt said she would keep the two special cats for her until next week and suggested that Wednesday around noon would be a good time to come pick up her new meowing companions. The woman said "okay" and walked slowly to her car, snorting and wheezing, with a bewildered expression. I told my aunt that she had finally crossed the line. She said to me, 'I just gave a very lonely woman a purpose for getting up in the morning and the opportunity to feel needed and loved. I refuse to apologize for my kind deed.'   "Luke, always check your truck before you leave her place. Aunt Tilly is not only determined, but sneaky. By the way, how is your son doing?"

"Drake is a great kid. He loves going to daycare. They tell me he gets along with everyone and the other kids seem drawn to him. Thanks for asking. Maybe sometime we could play a few rounds of tennis, like perhaps some Sunday afternoon? Drake would like watching."

Brooksie looked down at her feet, hesitated and then responded, "Maybe someday we could do that. Does Drake's mother also play tennis?"

"I don't know. I am Drake's foster dad and soon hope to be his adoptive father. It's quite a story. Perhaps you would like to hear about it sometime?"

"I'm sorry about being so nosey. I think it is fantastic you are adopting a deserving child. I have thought about doing the same thing one day. How difficult is it to become a single foster parent?"

"Not easy, but certainly not impossible. Somewhat time consuming and most definitely rewarding. I'll gladly go into the details when you want more information.

"I will email you an itemized statement, but I can give you a ball park figure of two thousand dollars and it will take about four days to complete the entire project. I want to take you to Marshall's Nursery so you can pick out the plants you would like placed in the raised flower garden. So the planting won't be finished until you have chosen what you want and they will be planted within a day or two of our trip to the nursery. My estimate does not include the plants you choose."

"The price sounds fair and I'm surprised how quickly it will be done. Where do I sign?"

"Print off my email and sign. I'll pick it up later. Let me know when you have time on a Sunday for Drake and me on the courts."

"I'll do that. Please let me know when you are going to start out in back so I can lock up the cats and dogs. I am also interested in learning more how you went about becoming a foster parent when we both have more time."

"I'll call the day before I'm going to start work on your back yard. Maybe you could meet me for coffee and I can give you more details about the fostering process."

"I'd be glad to meet for coffee. I could pick your brain about fostering. Thanks again for fixing my yard up so quickly. Good-bye Luke."

She watched his old beat up truck snort and wheeze going down the driveway. Distractedly she zigzagged around the backyard unaware of the trail of dogs and one cat following close behind. *There is something so appealing to me about Luke and it's not just physical. I feel guilty and yet I've done nothing wrong. I love many things about Marino, but I can see trouble coming. I hate confrontation. I know in my heart we would be making a mistake staying together if we continue to disagree on such important issues.*

Finally, noticing the gang of wagging tails including Samson the cat who considers himself a dog, she sat down and lovingly embraced them all and spoke out loud, "loving you all is so easy and being loved in return is always without conditions."

CHAPTER TWENTY-FIVE

**Nobody holds a good opinion of a man
who has a low opinion of himself.**
Anthony Trollope - *Orley Farm*

Session 7

Brooksie had asked Tony and Lucinda to meet in her office one half hour before group was to begin. Once the three of them were in the room, door closed, Brooksie summarized what Loreli had told her. She described Loreli as cheerful, well-groomed, animated and not at all depressed looking. She passed on the information Loreli had shared with her about her concern for Jason's mood swings."

"I'm quoting Loreli now, 'Sometimes I'm afraid for myself and the next day I'm afraid for Jason. I know something about suicide and I'm wondering if he is thinking about killing himself?'

"I called the clinic's attorney and Detective Marino and shared what I could with them. Both Jason and Loreli are presenting different pictures of each other, almost opposite descriptions. It doesn't make sense to me. I suggested she see a therapist and we talked about safety issues for her."

"What is going on with these two people?" asked Lucinda. "Jason has never appeared as someone seriously depressed. I see him as sad, but he is always well groomed, verbalizes his feelings well and sounds like he is trying to make his marriage work. After all, he is the one who signed up for this group."

"That reminds me," said Brooksie. "Loreli told me she knew about Jason coming to group almost from the beginning. She said she found a receipt from the clinic in his clothes. Apparently, she has known since the first or second session, but never said anything. Feels like Twilight Zone, weird and upsetting. Is one lying? Maybe both."

"I guess we are on high alert for observing Jason," Tony remarked. "What did Detective Marino have to say after what you told him, Brooksie?"

"He hasn't gotten back to me yet. I expect to hear something tomorrow for sure. I will call you both at home if he has something of significance. He may also have some news about Melissa. It seems there was a footprint found by one of the windows at Melissa's home. I forgot to pass this on a few days back, when Marino told me. Maybe this will be important later on.

"Our group is beginning to gather. We better finish this conversation later."

Once the members finished chatting and found their seats, Lucinda said, "Today begins our seventh session, one more to go. We want you all to focus on your strengths. What character traits do you bring into a relationship that are positive? Traits that you feel good about, maybe even receive compliments about. Brooksie would you start us off? It might help to have some examples?"

"Sure I'll be happy to speak of some of my positive traits, at least I consider them to be positive. I'm mostly kind, laugh loudly, often and especially at myself. I've learned to hold back on judgments and feel compassion for others and myself. I'm an advocate for people of all ages and animals, a good listener, and I don't believe in quitting, only in retreating and taking another path."

Ruth spoke up, "I'm loyal, a good cook, okay in emergency situations. I like to do nice things for others. I think I could have been a good nurse or maybe a nurse's aide." Tony smiled at Ruth and gave a thumbs up.

"I'm goal directed, self-sufficient, generous at times, some find me interesting, good with money and can't be bullied," offered Jason. "I have my own company and support ten employees. Seven are CPAs, plus three secretaries. I am considerate of my employees and interested in their private lives as well as their work lives."

"I want to take my turn now," said Shannon. "I'm trustworthy, strong both emotionally and physically, plus faithful to a fault. I'm a survivor and a good friend."

Gage shifted in his seat and said, "Guess I'll take a crack at this. I'm also faithful, like you Shannon. I love my kids and wife. I'm willing to learn about myself and make changes. I'm playful, a good house builder, a self-taught handy man of many trades."

"I'm glad to have this opportunity to share this," offered Melika. "I've learned in these sessions that I'm brave, never thought of myself as courageous, but I am. I am also organized, a good cook and seamstress. I am a doer. I follow through with plans and finish what I start. I'm a painter, not great, but I like putting the beauty of nature on canvas."

"Today, I can say I'm a better man than my Dad in every way," offered Kent. "I want to tell you guys that Marlene and I are back together. We had a conference here Monday night which included Brooksie, Lucinda, Tony, and the private investigator. I was finally able to tell my wife about my past. It turns out my sister-in-law had paid this private investigator to check up on my background. His report included the criminal history of my father, my pitifully weak mother, and my first loveless marriage. Turns out the secrets I kept for such a long time were the cause of my problems. I'm relieved to find out that none of the past mistakes make any difference to Marlene. She really does love me just the way I am in the present. I'm on cloud nine, but my feet are firmly planted on solid ground.

"I'm good at compromising. I like to please people, especially women and sometimes men. I have become more thoughtful, even wise once in a while. I love my wife unconditionally, deeply and will fight to make our marriage work. This is a surprise to me, but I can feel some sadness for my weak mother. My anger is not so all-consuming any more. She didn't protect me or herself from the tyrant, but I don't really know much about how she was treated as a kid."

"Sounds like you're beginning to feel compassion for your mother," observed Cecelia. "I want to congratulate you on being reunited with your wife. A lesson to us all about the harm that secrets can bring about."

Cecelia continued, "I'm a finisher. I finish whatever I start. I always do my best. I'm honest, true blue, sincere and generous. I'm told I have a good throaty laugh. Not sure if that is good or bad."

All of the other participants congratulated Kent. Jason shook his hand, Tony and Gage both gave him a bear hug as did the women.

"You have given me hope for my own situation Kent, and I'm happy for you and a little bit envious," said Gage.

"Don't give up man, keep on trying to find ways that will bring you and your wife closer."

"I'm ready to take a turn now," said Lucinda. "I have become my own hero. I no longer allow someone else to hold me hostage or make me feel guilty for trying to take care of myself. I'm worth knowing. I'm a friend, trustworthy and can play a pretty wicked game of tennis."

Lucinda quickly glanced over at Tony, who winked at her. Lucinda's cheeks lit up and she looked away.

"Looks like I'm the last one standing," said Tony, smiling. "I'm reliable, genuine, caring, hard working, fair and have a good sense of humor. I try always to be a good dad to my precious daughter. Lastly I'm a damn good cabinet maker."

"Everyone has had an opportunity to speak of their positive traits, next we want all to think about what kind of support you have outside these walls," stated Lucinda. We have one more session to go. We want you prepared when conditions or situations arise that cause concern or in need of decisions. We are going to use the blackboard again. I'll write down any words that come to mind from any of you. Brooksie would you please be the first one?"

"Happy to. My aunt and uncle, friends and co-workers, often they are the same."

Shannon said, "My son and my best friend, Marsha."

Gage offered, "The staff, Mark, a guy I fish with, plus Roberto and Josh, two of my crew and of course, Gina."

Kent smiling his sexy dimpled grin added, "Marlene, the staff, Mr. Edwards the private investigator, all of you in this group and I plan to widen my circle of friends. Marlene doesn't need to be my sole support, just my soul mate.

"I feel like a kid on Christmas morning after a generous visit from Santa. All my wishes have come true.

"Rayana, my sister-in-law from hell, really hurt Marlene. As much as I dislike Rayana I wish there could be some peace between them. Marlene is such a forgiving person that her sister would only have to apologize and Marlene would feel so much better. Although I would never trust her sister again, not in this life. I would be courteous out of respect for Marlene."

Tony validated Kent's distrust of Rayana, "I would agree with you Kent. I, too, would be very watchful and probably suspicious of Rayana for a long time."

Jason also recommended that Kent and Marlene watch their backs. "I'm curious about Mr. Edwards. How did your sister-in-law find him?"

"I'm not sure. I just assumed she looked in the Yellow pages under private detectives or whatever. I can get his number for you if you'd like."

"No. That won't be necessary. I was just curious. My support will come from this staff and all of you. I like my employees, but I have kept a professional distance from them. There are two men, both CPAs that I feel I could confide in if I had to. Belinda is one of my secretaries. She has been with me for more than fifteen years and is sort of a mother to me, at least she tries to mother me. She is close to sixty and loves to give me advice. In a pinch I guess I could consider her a friend and partial confidant. I've shared more in this group then I have to anyone in my entire life."

Brooksie suggested it would take a little practice to share feelings when your emotional life was closed off for so long, or better said, closed in.

"My support will come from my parents, several close friends, this clinic's staff and all of you. Also my partner in the office plus one of the dental hygienists. She is a great listener and not prone to gossip or rumors," shared Cecilia.

"My turn," said Ruth. "I know I'm the Bible thumper here, but God is my first choice. Then I can say next is the staff, the people in this group, and two of my friends from church. That's all I can think of. My parents are not on this list. Hopefully all of my children will one day like me a little better. Tony you really made me feel better about myself, about my cooking and other stuff."

"I meant every word I said. I'm truly grateful I've had this opportunity to get to know you a little more."

"For me you can put on the board, friends, certain relatives, some of the volunteers I work with at the thrift store, my doctor and her nurse and lastly, I don't mean last on my list, I would definitely call everyone in the room," shared Melika.

"Our time is up for today. One more session to go," added Brooksie. "Next week we will again focus on personal support systems, individual goals and steps to get there and whatever any of you want to bring up. You all have the phone numbers of your facilitators and the other members, call if you need to. There is no such thing as a stupid question. See you next week."

Debriefing:

Lucinda started very quickly after the others left the room, "Jason does not look or sound depressed today or in fact never has since group one. What is going on with him and his wife?"

"It's a mystery to me too," responded Brooksie. "Maybe one or both of them are simply great actors, but what would be the purpose of misleading us? One way to clear this up would be to ask Jason if he would like to invite his wife to come and meet with the three of us.

"My question would be about safety. I don't know whose safety to be concerned about. I think I should ask both Detective Marino and Detective Swain their opinions. They have dealt with a number of domestic violence cases.

Tony agreed to Brooksie's suggestion concerning the detectives.

"I'll call Marino today and get some kind of answer or advice and get back with the two you."

CHAPTER TWENTY-SIX

Beauty is in the eye of the beholder.
Margaret Wolfe Hungerford. - *Molly Bawn*

A striking, spun-gold, blonde-headed woman looking to be in her early thirties, walked into the Whitefall Police Station. She moved gracefully to the desk and asked to speak with Detective Marino. All eyes in the room are fixed on the 5' 9" stunningly beautiful woman. She had the walk of a female well aware of her effect on onlookers.

Detective Marino walked toward her with his hand extended, "You must be Loreli Woods. Thanks for being on time."

Lorelie followed him back to his office and said, "I would appreciate a glass of water detective, if you don't mind."

"No problem, Mrs. Woods. Would you rather have something besides water? We have coffee, tea or soft drinks."

"No thank you, water will be fine. I have to watch my figure, you know."

"Trust me, you are not the only one watching your figure." The detective pushed a button on the wall and asked that a cold bottle of water with a glass be brought to his office.

In less than five seconds, two uniformed men arrived, one was holding a bottle of water and the other carried the glass.

"Sorry about the gawking. You must be used to that Mrs. Woods," offered Marino.

"You don't need to apologize detective. It's always nice to be appreciated even if it is for something so superficial as one's appearance."

They sat across from each other at the small table.

"Please start wherever you would like regarding your concerns. I would like your permission to tape our conversation. I will be taking down a few notes as well."

"That will be fine, detective. I don't know what Miss Everett has told you so far and I don't want to waste your time by repeating the same information."

"Miss Everett has told me nothing because it would be an issue of confidentiality and she honors everyone's privacy."

"In that case, I will start by saying my husband's behavior has changed toward me for the last five months or so. I sadly admit I'm unhappy and becoming more and more afraid of him. The problem seemed to start when I told him I wanted to get pregnant. Our relationship has gone downhill since then.

"When we got married, he told me he had never been married before. I really didn't know much about him. Guess I didn't feel it was necessary. He didn't talk much about his past. So I thought it was the first marriage for both of us. We didn't talk about children, but I assumed he wanted them, eventually. We had lots of fun! We traveled some and he was very generous with his money. He would buy me gifts, some expensive and others sweet.

"Our life together was great. Now everything is different. I'm embarrassed to say this, but even our sex life has changed. He wants rough sex which truly scares me. He was never like this before. I'm feeling like a prisoner in my own home. He seldom leaves me alone except when he goes to work or to the Grief Clinic on Thursday evenings. I overheard him tell the old, senile lady who lives next door that I'm depressed and asked her to try to cheer me up. His behaviors are becoming stranger with every passing week. I don't know what to do or who to turn to."

"Does he know you have talked to Miss Everett or about your appointment with me here today?" asked the detective.

"I don't think so. I work out at the gym three or more times a week. And I run three miles most days. I do all of this at different times of the day. When I spoke with Miss Everett, Jason had an appointment with his attorney. Today he's at work, as usual."

"Do you have your own car and credit cards?" asked Marino.

"Yes. I have a car and credit cards as well as cash. I know he checks my charges. I caught him looking at my car miles a week ago. I don't think I can live this way much longer. I'm afraid to leave him, but I have to do something. I asked him if we could go to counseling and he became enraged by the suggestion. He said I was the one with the problem. He keeps denying his own depression. I'm not sure if I'm more afraid of him hurting himself or hurting me."

"Has your husband physically hurt you or made any verbal threats to your safety?"

"No, he has not hit me or anything like that. He frightens me by his irrational behavior and like I said, I don't know if he wants to hurt himself or me. I know he owns a gun and keeps it loaded in his locked desk."

"Is there anyone you know and trust that you could stay with for a while?"

"I have no family really, only a cousin who lives in Chicago and an old aunt who lives in London. I haven't had any contact with either of them for many years. The old gal is probably dead by now. I've never had many friends. Women always seem to be uncomfortable around me like I'm going to steal their man. Men have only one thing in mind. No offense. When I met Jason he was so different and I thought I finally had someone who really cared. He didn't just want to jump my bones, he wanted to take care of me."

A small tear found its way down her flawless cheek and dared not to spread her mascara.

Marino fumbled around, reaching for the Kleenex box on the table in front of them and awkwardly handed her a tissue. Loreli looks directly into his dark piercing eyes and then slowly looked away.

"I will file this report so there will be a record of your concerns. I hope you will keep aware of your husband's moods. If, for any reason, you become afraid of him, leave! Drive away if possible, and go to the nearest populated place, even a neighbor's house and dial 911 or use your cell phone."

They shook hands and walked out together from the station, which created a quietness again with gazes from all following the visitor. Marino accompanied her to her car, which was a pewter-colored jaguar. Loreli thanked him again and drove off.

CHAPTER TWENTY-SEVEN

Meet me half way,
You need the exercise.
Dr. Robert Anthony - *Think Again*

The weekend arrived bringing full sunshine. No clouds and the temperature climbed to the high sixty-degree mark. All of this promised by the weatherman, of course.

Brooksie busied herself with the usual tasks of feeding pets, washing clothes and doing a minimum of yard work.

The phone rang. Detective Marino was on the other end. "Hi hon, wanted to catch you before you got too busy running errands. I need to share some of what Loreli Woods told me. Do you have a minute?"

"Absolutely. What did she have to say?"

"Basically, she thinks her husband is very depressed and at times she thinks he may hurt himself. At other times she is afraid he will hurt her. She stated he is moody and has changed a great deal in the last six months.

"I gave her the usual information we give to all who make complaints of abuse and living in a violent home. 'The how to file a restraining order.' And I suggested other safety measures."

"Blake, does she strike you as a depressed, or abused woman?"

"I'm excited about the entire program. I'm going to let Tony look it over because he might have some suggestions from a male perspective.

"I also spoke with Rachael and she is anxious to get this project underway. She's been working on several grants. She has also contacted a local Soroptimist club and said the president of the club sounded very interested in sponsorship."

"I believe something very good is rising from the cremated ashes of Maureen. Sharon is amazing! She's the perfect person to teach others coming from hellish childhoods to make respectful and constructive choices.

"The email requested another get together at the prison one or two months from now. That will be good timing for me, how about you?"

"I will plan for it and let Rachael know about the time. See you tomorrow. By the way, do you want to ride with Tony and me?"

"Thanks Lucinda, but Marino and his partner are going to pick me up. I'm kind of glad Blake and I won't be alone. I'm feeling more uncomfortable about our future together. He is set against our working with Sharon at the prison and I don't see any wiggle room for either of us.

"How about you and Tony?"

"The more I'm with him the more I like him. I've never known such a kind and thoughtful man. In fact, I never before did I believe I deserved anyone this good. Mom's brainwashing has done a number on me.

"Brooksie I'm falling hard for him and it scares the shit out of me. My history concerning romance has been a disaster. I can still hear Mom whispering in my ear, 'you mess up every relationship.' I'm trying hard to shut out her nasty and hurtful words, but a part of me whispers, what if she is right?"

"Your mother did a number on you years ago, but you are older and wiser now and have seen the cruel, selfish motives behind your mother's behaviors and words. Now you get to make choices. Your choice of what to believe about yourself. You are a beautiful woman inside and out. You are kind, hardworking, committed to the helping profession and not for financial rewards that's for sure. You are a friend, an exceptional therapist, tons of fun and a far better skier than me.

"I hope you and Tony take time to get to know one another and discover all there is to appreciate about each other."

"See you later Brooksie and thanks."

CHAPTER TWENTY-EIGHT

**What we once enjoyed and
deeply loved we can never lose,
for all that we love deeply
becomes part of us.**
Helen Keller

The memorial

Most everyone who was invited from the staff pulled up in the parking lot about the same time. Shaun was already there, standing on the sand and staring out at the slow rolling waves gently washing on to the shore. One lone seagull stood nearby like a sentry.

Anita rushed up to Brooksie and gave her a hearty embrace. Brad joined his sister and shook hands all around.

Tony said, "I'm truly happy to meet both of you." He was looking at Anita and Brad. "Anita, I understand you are doing well in school and Brad, you have a new job, is that right?"

"Not exactly," answered Brad. I'm in training for the fire department. I still have a few months of tests to go, interviews and other hoops to jump through. Then, hopefully, I'll be assigned to a station and can start saving the world."

"I'm so proud of him," responded Anita. "We are both on wonderful career paths." Looking at Tony she continued, "Lucinda told us you're one fantastic volunteer. You are both insightful and compassionate. She also told us you write children's books and are a master furniture maker."

"I wouldn't call myself a master of anything, just a simple cabinet maker. I would like to build my own house some day. I love working with my hands."

"Tony, I didn't know you wanted to take on such a huge project like a house. You're always surprising me," said Lucinda.

"I like surprising you."

"What a fine plan. If you need a referral for a landscaper when that time comes let me know. My uncle referred me to someone who seems to be excellent and affordable," offered Brooksie.

"I'll sure think about that, and thanks."

"What's this Brooksie, you've hired a landscaper to do what?" asked Marino.

"I'm having some work done both in the front and the back. It's a jungle and it's too much work for me. Uncle Joe recommended him."

"You could've asked me to help you."

"You have enough to do and I didn't think either of us was up to stone work. I knew you would help if I asked you. This way neither of us would have to kill ourselves."

Another car pulled up and Jason, Kent, Maureen and Gage all climbed out. Introductions were made all around including Shaun who had timidly joined the group. Kent joyfully introduced his wife to all and appeared as proud as a father of a newborn.

Lastly, the four female members of the divorce group drove up and parked. More introductions followed and the mourners moved onto the sandy beach. Most removed their shoes and carried them in their hands.

Shaun led them to the water's edge and asked all to form a circle. This was accomplished silently. Only the soft sound of the surf broke the quietness. They all took hold of their neighbor's hand and dropped their shoes beside them.

Shaun's lips began to quiver when he spoke. "We are here, Melissa, at one of your favorite places, to say we miss you, I miss you. I hope you know I loved you. You have gone on and I'm left behind. Not sure what to do next. I don't know what else to say except good-bye for now."

He wiped his face with his sleeve and asked if anyone wanted to hold the container with Melissa's ashes before he released them into the gentle ocean waves.

Ruth asked if she could offer a short prayer before he passed the urn around.

Shaun said, "Please do."

Ruth started the Lord's Prayer and everyone joined in.

The urn was passed by Shaun to Jason who was standing next to him. Jason nearly dropped the container saying, "I'm sorry I've never held anyone's ashes before. Thanks Melissa for letting me show you pictures of my beautiful wife and for listening to me whine. You were so patient and kind."

Kent was next and said good-bye and passed the urn to the next person. So it went with each one saying something. Tears flowed like a light rainfall from most everyone.

Brooksie was the last one holding the ashes before reaching Shaun. She said, "Melissa you were a fantastic secretary and a woman who loved life. You were always cheerful and made the office a welcoming and healing place for all. We are seeking justice for you my friend and we wish you more great adventures in your new place. See you."

Shaun then took the top off the vessel and walked into the water a few feet, many followed. When the next wave kissed his toes he let the ashes fall and he blew them a kiss.

The ceremony ended. After a quick conference, the majority decided they would meet for lunch at the Fish House.

As they walked back to their cars, Lucinda said, "I have always avoided attending funerals. Half the time the minister presiding didn't even know the deceased. This was the most meaningful service I've ever been to. I know there is always value participating in the funeral for those left behind, but this was really beautiful. I could almost feel Melissa enjoying it herself."

Marino whispered to Brooksie he had just received a call so he and Swain needed to return to the office right away. Brooksie said okay and she would get a ride with someone.

The detectives drove off and Brooksie asked Shaun if she could ride with him to the restaurant.

"Absolutely. I would like the company. I have something to ask you anyway."

Brooksie climbed into Shaun's older Ford that displayed several dents and scratches. She was hoping they weren't a result of his driving skills.

Once they were underway, Shaun said, "I had a strange feeling when that man who was standing next to me said something about the pictures of his beautiful wife. I remembered Melissa telling me the night she was murdered something about pictures and that whoever she saw in the bathroom looked much like some pictures she was shown at the office by some client."

"Are you saying she saw someone in the ladies room at The Barn that looked like pictures she had been shown at the office.?"

"Yes. Now I remember Melissa had just come from the rest room when she said something about seeing a woman she shouldn't have. I didn't really take what she told me very seriously."

"Did you tell the detectives what you just told me?"

"No. I didn't even remember it until now. I've been torn up about Melissa and not thinking real straight. Should I tell them now?"

"Yes! After lunch you can drive us to the station and you can tell the detectives what you just told me. Okay?"

"Okay. Anything to help them find her killer. You know I really did love her. I know we only were together for about six months, but she was so special. I was happy with her and I believe I made her happy, too."

"I'm truly sorry about your loss. She definitely seemed happy and that may very well have been due to you," offered Brooksie.

"That's kind of you to say. Maybe we were good for each other. I just can't get my head around the fact someone murdered her. Maybe I'll feel better when the maniac is caught or killed, but I don't think I'll ever really be one hundred percent."

"Shaun you may have some difficult days, months and maybe even years ahead of you, but you do have a future. You had a life before Melissa and now you have a life without her. Now you know how good it can be when you are with the right person. I don't believe for one minute there is only one right person for us on this big planet. Give yourself time to work through your grief and then who knows what adventure awaits you."

CHAPTER TWENTY-NINE

**In the midst of winter I found at last
there was within myself an invincible summer.**
Albert Camus - *Winter Grief Summer Grace*

Brooksie placed a call inviting Jason and his wife to come to the office for a joint appointment with Lucinda, Tony and herself.

Jason thought that was a good idea and would tell Loreli about the appointment.

Brooksie and Jason agreed to Tuesday at 5:30 p.m. at the office.

Tuesday rolled around and the three facilitators were milling around waiting for Jason and Loreli to show. Jason came through the office door fifteen minutes late.

"So sorry I'm late. I talked myself blue in the face trying to get Loreli to come with me, but she cried and said she was feeling poorly. She finally agreed she would come next week.

"I'm beginning to consider the possibility our marriage may be over. She doesn't seem willing to try at all. Am I blind or am I a stupid fool? I wonder if she ever loved me. When I put the brakes on her spending everything changed and went to pot, and not the smoking kind, either. Where do I go from here?

Brooksie contemplated what to say next. She glanced at Lucinda and Tony and they both had that 'what now, look.' She decided to lay her cards on the table and pay close attention to Jason's responses and reactions. "Jason you and your wife have painted very different pictures of each other. I'm going to share some things that may surprise or even shock you."

Brooksie again looked over at Lucinda who nodded and raised her hand with the okay sign.

"Your wife called me and asked me to meet her at the public library. Said she wanted to talk about her situation. I told her I couldn't confirm your attendance at the clinic, explaining confidentiality rules. She told me I wouldn't need to say anything she just wanted to get some things off her chest.

"She did not fit the description of someone depressed. In fact, she was wearing a bright colored, form-fitting outfit. Her makeup was flawless and her body language screamed self-confidence. She gave the impression she was well aware of her good looks and great figure.

"Her story was not at all like yours. She claimed you are the one who is depressed. You are, at times, very moody and she was afraid of what you might do to yourself and what you might do to her. She added that when you get angry she becomes more concerned for her own safety."

Jason's breathing was becoming shallow, like he was holding his breath. His face paled and registered disbelief.

"Do you want me to continue?"

"Yes, but could I have some water first?"

Tony got up and brought Jason a cold bottle of water. When he handed it to Jason, he noticed his hand was shaking.

Brooksie continued, "Your wife went to see Detective Marino at the Whitefall Police Station and told a similar tale to the detective."

"Now do you understand why we wanted the two of you together to tell your stories?"

"I can't believe what I'm hearing. Is my wife crazy? Could she have two personalities?. I don't know how to make any sense out of what I have just heard. Everything I said about Loreli was true. She doesn't dress up, she stays in her pajamas or nightgowns most of the day. She wears no makeup around me. I can't believe we are talking about the same person.

"I am sad at times, but never for long. I have never considered hurting myself and never would I hurt her or any human being. What is going on with her? Is she mentally ill?

Jason stood up and walked in circles around the room, He wiped his forehead, took off his glasses and rubbed his eyes. A few minutes passed, he fell into his seat like he weighed a ton. "Have I ever looked and sounded so depressed that it gave you the impression I was considering suicide or hurting someone else?"

"No. You have sounded sad and frustrated at times, but I've never thought you were capable of violence of any kind," answered Lucinda.

Tony responded with similar impressions.

"Have you ever lost your temper with Loreli?" asked Brooksie.

"Never. I'm not a violent man. In fact, I've been told by a few folks how even tempered I am. I have simply felt confused and at a loss as to how to help Loreli."

"Jason, take a moment to think before you answer. Have you ever talked about suicide with Loreli or with anyone?"

"No. I've had my sad times, especially when I was a young boy and my parents were off seeing the world. They didn't want me around them much. Their disinterest in me hurt me, but I was never in so much pain that I couldn't see a future for me. I made up my mind to be financially successful and working hard helped me to feel okay about myself. Or maybe I'm too shallow to get depressed. I've never really expected much from life, at least not personal happiness. I've always been satisfied with my job, proud of my company and employees. That was enough until Loreli showed up. I couldn't believe she was interested in me. I have experienced great joy with her. Now what am I to do?

"I don't know anything about her past. Maybe I need to simply ask her why she acts one way with me and differently with others. What if I confront her and she turns all psychotic? Maybe I will say nothing and wait and see if she will come with me next week to see you all.

"Now I'm really sad, not suicidal, just sad because it looks like there is no us anymore, no Loreli and me. Maybe there never was. I wanted her to love me, to be in love with me. I wanted to feel lovable. If only to prove my parents wrong. I know I'm not the golden ring everyone would like to grab, but I'm not a booby prize either. I do have some good traits to bring to a relationship. I've learned that in our group work.

"What do you three think I should do? Jason held eye contact with each one without blinking. I'm at a loss."

"Is there one employee you are close to, one you have a great respect for and one you would be comfortable confiding in?" asked Tony.

"Belinda, my secretary has been with me the longest. She has been like a caring mother to me, even though we are about the same age. She is completely trustworthy and knows how to keep private things private. She did try to advise me not to marry Loreli so soon after we started dating. She wanted me to get some background information on her. I blew off her suggestions. Now I must swallow my undeserved pride and fess up."

Brooksie added, "Perhaps you could go to a hotel tonight to give yourself time to assimilate what you heard today and then decide what your next step will be."

"I can do that. I'll call Loreli from the hotel and tell her we need to talk and plan to see her tomorrow. I do need some time to chew on what I've heard tonight.

"I appreciate the time you are spending trying to help me. I'm sorry this has gotten so complicated. Actually I'm glad we have one more session to go so I can share all of this with people who care about me. I do feel close to the members, closer to some especially to Kent and now his sweet wife. Cecelia and I also have a rapport. I respect her a great deal for how she is handling the betrayal by someone she loved. Maybe there is a lesson there for me.

"Thank you all. See you Thursday evening."

Jason left the office and the three watched him through the window as he climbed into his luxury car and drove off.

"Can we go for something to eat before we all go home? asked Lucinda.

"Okay by me. I'll call my child's sitter and let her know I'll be home in about an hour and to put Katrina to bed."

"I'm not hungry, but I'm too wound up to go home" said Brooksie. "Do you guys want to go to the Table Talk or someplace else?"

"Table Talk sounds great," agreed Tony.

CHAPTER THIRTY

**I have always thought the actions of men
the best interpreters of their thoughts.**
John Locke - *An Essay Concerning
Human Understanding.*

Session Eight

It was Thursday, close to 6 p.m. Kent and Shannon walked in together. Both smiled and looked happy. Kent filled a cup of coffee and handed it to Shannon.

Cecelia, Ruth and Melika entered the room almost at the same time, except they couldn't all fit through the door at the exact same time which brought peals of laughter.

Melika could be heard saying, "That is a fantastic and generous plan, Cecelia."

"I don't know about that," responded Ruth."I would be mighty embarrassed, but I must say it sounds exciting. Are you sure you can afford it Cecelia?"

"I would not have offered if I couldn't afford it. It would bring me much pleasure. We just need to agree on a date and time. It will require one entire day to get everything accomplished."

Shannon moved next to the women and stated, "What a great time we will have. Cecelia, you are so generous. This will be the best gift I've ever been given with the exception of the birth of my son. I'm sure this will be far more fun than that was." A chorus of laughter from all four women echoed in the hallway.

Gage arrived just in time to hear Shannon's remark. "Guess I missed the punch line." He had a sparkle in his eyes and was handsomely dressed.

Lucinda spoke up, "Okay ladies time to sit and share what all the excitement is about."

Ruth spoke up, still trying to contain her laughter, "Cecelia has made a most wonderful offer for us ladies. She is paying for the four of us to go to a spa for a day and have a make-over. I've never had a massage or had anyone fuss over me before. I'm nervous about it, but really looking forward to it. Hope I don't become one of those snobbish women afterwards. Maybe I won't want to do dishes anymore because it would mess up my nails." She began to laugh again in earnest and didn't even try to control her glee.

Shannon and Melika shared their happiness and anticipation of the coming full day of pampering.

"I've already begun to eat more nutritiously. Good food and exercise are part of my plan for my metamorphosis. Who knows what's around the corner, maybe a date?" said Shannon with a twinkle in her eye.

Brooksie looked at her watch. It was 6:15 and Jason had not yet shown up. She excused herself, went to call him from her office. No answer. She left a message and returned to the group room.

"We're going to get started," said Brooksie. Hopefully Jason will show soon. I called his home and left a message since he didn't answer. He's probably on his way.

"This evening we are planning to go over your support backups again, any pressing concerns, goals, insights and any news you want to share."

Cecelia began, "I would like to propose something for everyone before we get down to business.

"The ladies, including myself are going to have a make-over day four weeks from now. We would like to suggest a ninth session to be a show and tell, to show off our new hairdos and whatever else is new. An informal time to check on each one and see how everybody is doing."

"What a great idea," said Gage. I would like to bring my wife and show her off as well. My great news is we're working together. We have an appointment with a marriage counselor next week. I have apologized to Gina for my selfishness and told her how proud I am of her and will support all of her endeavors from now on. I was even able to tell her about my bad feelings regarding my parents' parallel marriage and my fears that we had been heading that way. We talked for hours and cried together. She told me she loved me and had truly been missing us."

Cheers and praise were heard from each one in the room. Gage was beaming and graciously received the many hugs and handshakes.

"I might as well jump in with my good news! Marlene and I are back together as man and wife. It seems my wicked sister-in-law had hired a private investigator and he uncovered my unsavory past and gave her a written report. Not like I'm a criminal, but sadly my father is. He's in prison for deceiving and stealing a great deal of money from his clients. Those were people who trusted him with their life savings.

"My weak mother and I were shunned by family and friends alike. We became your basic street people. Even spent a short time living in our car. I won't bore you with every sordid detail except to say I became one very angry adolescent and teenager. Made lots of bad choices. Eventually I hooked up with an older, wealthy widow. We were not a match made in heaven, but we were cut from the same cloth, both damaged material. I became the trophy 'wife,' her show piece.

"She was actually very good to me and understood my bedrock fear of poverty and shame. She had a damaged heart from childhood and she died suddenly a few years after we were married. I was suspected of causing her death probably because I was sole heir to her large estate. Took a long time for her old medical records to be located by the police. The records showed that she'd had scarlet fever as a child which damaged her heart and eventually caused her early death. She never wanted anyone to know about her heart problems. She didn't want to appear flawed in any way. I was eventually cleared of all suspicion except by her friends.

The estate was settled later after her death. Then I found myself a wealthy man. I went sort of crazy and blew through the majority of the undeserved inheritance. Eventually I stopped self-destructing and was about out of money so I returned to construction part-time and sold real estate on the weekend.

"That is how I met Marlene. I sold her a beach house. Didn't take long for me to fall in love with her. She was the first woman I ever loved. She made me want to be a better man, someone I could actually respect.

"Obviously I still had much to learn because I kept my past a secret from her. I was afraid if she knew the sordid facts about my past she wouldn't want anything to do with me. It was only in the last few years before I met Marlene that I started to take responsibility for my actions.

"Marlene said I have come so far from the hell hole I was raised in and that makes her proud of me."

At this point Gage was wiping away glistening drops from under his eyes. He wasn't the only one in the room reaching for a tissue.

"Kent you've had a trial by fire life and you've come out way ahead," said Cecelia. "Have you visited your father since he was incarcerated?"

"No, Cecelia. I don't even know if either of my parents are alive. Maybe one day I will look up my mother. I have no intention of ever looking up my father."

"Now I'm trying to be less churchie Kent, but I've got to say forgiveness isn't about you helping your parents. It is to help the one who has been wronged. You would be the one who would benefit," offered Ruth.

"Thanks Ruth I know you mean well. We both had similar childhood experiences. At least that is how I see it. Our parents made us feel worthless and ashamed. I turned my hurt into anger and made bad choices. You turned your hurt into anger at your husband and tried to compensate by an overactive church participation. Hope I'm not offending you. I just see a comparison. I see both of us have struggled for a long time trying to overcome our sense of inferiority."

"I'm not offended. I see us more like beauty and the beast. Me the beast of course," said Ruth.

"Whoa. I'm thinking more of the ugly duckling and now you are both becoming magnificent swans," added Tony.

"I like your fairy tale better than mine," responded Ruth.

"I can throw one out also for you Ruth and that is Cinderella. Your brother was admired, spoiled and getting all the love and praise while you were scrubbing floors and doing everything possible to please your parents. We all know how that story ends," said Melika.

"Melika, what plans do you have for the near future?" asked Brooksie.

"I'm not going to accept any more calls at work from my ex. He can call the children at reasonable hours and they can call him. If this doesn't work, I'm changing my number. If he threatens to kill himself, I will repeat to him only one more time that he needs to see a counselor, but if he decides to commit suicide, I would tell him that is his decision. The choice is his. I will also emphasize to my kids that all people, young and old, make choices and they are responsible for the choices they make. I will encourage them more often and I will make more time for them to express their feelings and concerns. I'll even share some of mine with them."

She took several deep breaths and continued, "It was so good to hear those words coming from me. Self-pity is the opposite of acting responsibly. I want better for my children."

Lucinda addressed Shannon, "What plans do you have for your tomorrows?"

"For one, I plan to accept more offers from my co-workers to go to movies, bowling or even weekend ski trips when asked. I'm thinking of joining a service club. There is a Kiwanis Club that meets close to where I work. They do lots of projects helping children and adults. Years back, a friend of Danny's parents invited me to a Kiwanis meeting, but of course my husband told me they were a group of do-gooders and it would be an added expense. So I wimped out.

"I woke up this morning and actually felt excited about tomorrow. I'm so looking forward to our make-over day. Cecelia, you are so wonderful for doing this. You have no idea how lucky I feel and how much I appreciate your kindness."

"My pleasure, I assure you. I too, am looking forward to a day of pure self-indulgence with my friends," answered Cecelia.

"Do you think that a day at this spa place is all about vanity?' asked Ruth, addressing no one in particular.

"It's not about vanity, Ruth, it's about caring for oneself. Taking care of our bodies and souls is life affirming. Do you think God will love you less if you have pretty nails and an attractive hairdo?"

"Probably not. Each day I'm going to try to remember what I've learned from you all. I'm going to take more time fixing myself up in the morning. I want my kids to be proud of me and to bring friends to our house and not be embarrassed by me looking like an old hag.

"I'm even thinking about visiting my parents or maybe even inviting them to dinner. I would like to make my old-fashioned 'stick to the ribs' kind of meal. I can make two of my best pies and after dinner, tell my parents I respect and honor them because it is a commandment, even though they have hurt me many times by comparing me to my brother. I might even tell them that they don't need to send me anymore general birthday cards.

"We have only known each other for eight weeks, but you all have said nicer things about me in that short time. More than my folks have ever said in the last fifty years.

"I have done a decent job as a mother and you all have helped me to see that. I will always have to honor my parents, but I don't have to like them because of the way they treat me."

"Amen to that," said Tony.

All of the others encouraged Ruth to focus on her positive traits and skills. Shannon asked for a recipe for one of Ruth's pies and Melika asked for more details how to make a great Yankee pot roast.

Ruth was beaming ear to ear with the requests and new found importance and acknowledgements of her cooking expertise. Gage asked for the apple pie instructions. "I would love to surprise Gina and the kids with a great dessert one night. Make sure you write down all the details 'cause I'm not familiar with baking. Actually I can barely boil water."

Cecelia handed out the written directions to the spa with date and time. She then asked the staff what they thought about meeting in four weeks and everyone could bring guests including children, dates, partners, parents or whoever they wanted to.

Brooksie said it would be fine. Wednesday, Friday or Saturday at noon could work for her.

Lucinda said Wednesday or Saturday would be best for her and Tony agreed.

It was agreed upon that Saturday at noon would work and the place could be decided on later.

The Table Talk Cafe was mentioned as a possible place. The Book Ends book store which also has a lovely room with an outdoor large patio/garden area could be rented as well. Food could be catered or everyone could bring something to share.

"Marlene and I would love to take charge of renting and catering for this get together. If that is okay with you all?"

A moment of silence followed by clapping and cheering for the couple's generosity.

"Well, I guess that is a yes," said Kent. "Marlene will love organizing this special event."

"Sounds like we are going to have quite a party, a very festive reunion. I'll be glad to reserve the room at the bookstore and make sure we can set up tables for eating on the patio and garden area," offered Brooksie.

All agreed on the time, place and thanked Kent for his generous offer. Kent then asked Ruth if she would be willing to bring several of her homemade pies.

Ruth's smile was so wide it covered the bottom half of her face. "With pleasure. They will be my very best ones, that's for sure."

Brooksie said she would confirm the date and time with The Book Ends and only let the group know if there needed to be a change. The plans being settled, the group disbanded and Brooksie made another call to Jason's house. Still no one answered so she left another message.

This feels like deja vu. My heart is off to the races again. There has just got to be a simple explanation for Jason's absence.

CHAPTER THIRTY-ONE

Anger is one letter short of danger.
Anonymous

Five p.m. Thursday evening and Jason was getting ready to go to the last session of the divorce group. Loreli was dressed in her gym clothes and acting quite lovey dovey with him. She rubbed up against him in her practiced provocative way and offered him a drink of rum and coke saying she was feeling much better and wanted to celebrate their marriage. "I've been very happy being your wife. Sorry I've been out of sorts lately."

Loreli kissed him long and slowly with the unspoken promise of what would follow.

Jason hesitantly took the drink from her hand, they clinked glasses and both took swallows. She encouraged him to enjoy the libation and soon as he finished the last drop he told her they needed to talk.

She agreed as she was filling his glass again. She toasted to their future, but Jason said they should talk first then drink. He went on to tell her what Brooksie and Detective Marino had told him.

"What the hell is going on with you, Loreli. You've been saying I'm depressed and that you are afraid of me and for me. Did you really tell them I might hurt you or myself?"

"You spoiled everything. Our lives were going fine until you became Mr. Tightwad. You let me believe you had lots of money and liked spending it on me. I thought you wanted to keep me happy. You don't really think I married you for your looks or your personality. I've had a lot of fun and far better sex at the gym. You're no great lover."

Hateful words spewed from Loreli's mouth. Months of pent up resentment and anger came gushing out. She continued to tell him how much she detested him since the day of their wedding. She talked for another five minutes waiting for signs the drugs were taking effect on her confused mate. Her fevered stare was intense. She began to appear like a rabid, snarling dog, with her upper lip curled, showing her teeth. Her voice was raised several octaves, almost to a shrill.

"Why are you saying these things? Have you gone crazy? You look like a wild animal. You never answerrr... me. Di you saaay those thin.....g abou....me. I feel funny. wha....ts happ... ing? What was in drink? Loreli hel.... me." Perspiration appeared on his forehead and above his upper lip. His speech was slurred and he had trouble focusing.

Loreli was rummaging in a drawer while talking. Jason began to rub his eyes and placed a hand on top of the nearby chair to steady himself.

Awkwardly and with great effort he stood up and reached for Loreli when he saw the gun in her hand. "You're going to shoot me?" He stumbled, catching his foot at the edge of the rug, trying desperately to grab at the gun. Loreli backed away, Jason was falling toward her and she fired. Jason crumpled in place and didn't move. The rug under him turned bright red, Jason remained motionless.

Loreli quickly wiped her prints from the gun and placed it near Jason's left hand. He didn't appear to be breathing. She leaned in close and could not hear any sounds of respirations. When he fell, he hit his head on the coffee table and dropped into a fetal position.

She removed their drinking glasses and stuck them in the dishwasher and turned it on. She made one last look around, grabbed her gym bag, raced out the door, and headed for the gym and her alibi. She yelled "good-bye Jason," in case the busy body neighbor was watching or listening.

You poor man. You took an overdose, but couldn't wait for the drugs to take effect so you went for your gun and finished the job. You never were very patient. This was easier than getting rid of my first husband. He was much smarter and I had to be real clever. I got him though and he knew it those last few minutes.

Loreli spoke out loud while driving away, "Next time I'm going to pick a very old and decrepit geezer. I'm going to make sure I see his financial records before the senile bastard gets to wed and bed me."

CHAPTER THIRTY-TWO

Things are seldom what they seem.
Skim milk masquerades as cream.
W.S. Gilbert. H.M.S. - *Pinafore*

"I'm worried about Jason and Loreli," said Brooksie. "I want to drive over to his house and make sure they're okay. Jason was looking forward to this session. I've got a bad feeling. Something's not right."

"I agree," responded Lucinda. "Let's go now. What do you think Tony?"

"I'm not letting you two go alone that's for sure. In fact, Brooksie, I think we should let your detective friend know about our concerns. Maybe he will meet us."

"Good idea Tony. This is going to make him upset with me again, but he'll just have to get over it."

"I need to make a quick call to Katrina's sitter let her know I'll be late and for her to put my daughter to bed. Give me a minute."

"You don't think she'll have a problem with staying late?" asked Lucinda.

"No. She loves spending time with Katrina. Mrs. Long's time is her own. She has been a widow for more than three years and I believe taking care of my daughter has helped her through her tough grieving and lonely days and nights. She is a treasure and I believe she thinks the same of us."

Brooksie dialed the police department. Detectives Marino and Swain were off duty. She then was given Detective Sharp to talk with. Brooksie explained what the concerns were and asked if the detective could do a well check, in the next half an hour. The same time she and her friends would be at Jason's house.

The detective said she'd meet them there and asked Brooksie to wait for her before going to the front door.

The three drove up and parked in front of Jason's house. Lights are on in some areas of the house. No movement can be seen inside or out.

"How long do we have to wait here Brooksie?"

"The officer asked that we remain in our car until she arrived. We probably need to do what she asked. It only took us twenty minutes to get here and I asked the detective to meet us in half an hour. We shouldn't have much of a wait."

Fifteen minutes later, a police car pulled up and parked in front of the facilitator's car. Right behind the patrol car another unmarked car pulled up behind Tony's car and parked. Three officers alighted from the two cars.

A female officer approached Brooksie's car. "I'm Detective Sharp. The two officers and I will check out the place. Please remain in your car until I tell you otherwise."

One officer walked around to the back of the house while the detective and the other officer knocked on the door and rang the bell almost simultaneously. Nothing could be heard from the inside. The officer moved from the front door and looked into the living room. He quickly returned spoke to the detective and proceeded to kick the door in.

The three watching this, jumped out of their car and raced to the front steps. They were told, not too gently, to stay back.

Brooksie could partially see a person all crumpled up on the floor. "My God. Is that Jason?"

"Stay back. I have called for an ambulance."

"So he is alive then?" asked Tony.

"Yes, for now."

Sirens could be heard within a few minutes. The EMTs quickly took charge and placed Jason on a gurney after initially examining him.

Brooksie followed the gurney and asked if she could ride with Jason to the hospital because his wife was not available.

The attendant and the detective talked it over and Detective Sharp said, "Okay, but I need for the others to stay and give a quick report. I'll meet with the victim's doctor at the hospital shortly."

Tony told Brooksie to go ahead and they would catch up with her at the hospital. Brooksie wild-eyed, handed him the car keys. "See you soon."

Jason's moans were barely audible. The paramedic was busy doing his job. He started an IV, checked the wound and vitals and called ahead to the hospital with information about the condition of his patient, which didn't sound good to Brooksie.

Half way to the hospital Jason became momentarily lucid, and whispered, "Why did she?"

Brooksie asked, "Who shot you Jason?"

"Loreli, Loreli why?" He mumbled something else which neither Brooksie or the attendant could decipher. Jason drifted off. He was as pale as a ghost and barely breathing.

"Hold on Jason. We are almost to the hospital." Brooksie let out an uncontrollable sob.

The attendant suggested Brooksie keep talking to Jason and reassure him about his condition.

"Jason, this is Brooksie. Lucinda and Tony are praying for you. Please try to stay awake. Open your eyes, open them! I'm holding your hand. Squeeze my fingers, please Jason. We are almost there. The doctors are waiting for you. Please stay with us."

Brooksie's voice kept breaking up, fighting back tears she continued to try to get Jason's attention. Her heart was racing, mouth was dry like the desert in July, and she felt a tightness in her chest. *My God this can't be happening. What did I miss? How could Loreli fool so many?*

Upon arriving at the emergency room Jason, was rushed inside to the waiting staff.

Lucinda and Tony arrived shortly after. "How bad is it?" asked Lucinda.

"I don't know. He was barely breathing. I believe the EMT was busy trying to keep him alive. His vitals didn't sound good and by the expression on the EMT's face, Jason was in serious trouble."

A doctor came out to the waiting room after half an hour and asked for the wife.

"She's not here yet," answered Tony. "Can you tell us anything about his condition?"

"Is the wife coming?' asked the doctor. I am Dr. Williams and will be the operating surgeon. I would like to speak to his wife soon as possible."

Just then, Detective Sharp walked in, and told the doctor Mrs. Woods was on her way and would be arriving shortly.

"When she gets here please have me paged, " said the doctor.

"Will do, doctor," answered the detective. Five minutes later a wide-eyed Loreli raced through the emergency entrance looking like she was being chased by a pack of wolves.

"Where is he? I need to see him now!" she wailed. "What happened to him?. They told me he had been shot. He did it. He did what he threatened to do. I didn't believe him. He was fine when I left for the gym. He said he was going to the divorce group and would see me later. I told you he was depressed. I told you so," She rambled on to no one in particular.

Dr. Williams walked out and took Loreli aside. She was crying and pulling on her hair, but not enough to mess it up. Hanging onto the doctor's arm she got real close and told him to do everything possible to save her husband.

Dr. Williams didn't attempt to remove Loreli's hand on his arm. He spoke loud enough for most to hear, "He has lost a great deal of blood, and his vitals are dangerously low. He is receiving blood now and is being prepped for surgery."

Loreli was asked if her husband had any illnesses, like diabetes, heart problems or other health conditions plus any allergies. He also asked her if Jason had taken anything, any drug or alcohol this afternoon or evening. Loreli shook her head, indicating no. A nurse asked Loreli to follow her to the surgery waiting room. Brooksie accompanied Loreli and informed Detective Sharp that Lucinda and Tony must be brought to the same waiting room when they completed the interview with the police.

Just before entering the waiting room, Brooksie spotted Detective Marino coming down the hall. She told Loreli she would be right back and quickly stopped Marino before he entered the room. She pulled him aside and whispered, "I have to tell you something important. Walk around the corner with me."

As soon as they were out of earshot Brooksie told Marino what Jason said in the ambulance. "The attendant also heard what I did. If Jason lives, he will still be in danger from Loreli. You've got to protect him from her, Blake."

"It seems he was shot in the stomach just below the heart." said Marino. "I had a quick word with the doctor. Most people don't try to kill themselves with a bullet to the gut. Have you told anyone else what Jason told you?"

"No. Should I have?"

"Not yet. If she did try to kill him, we don't want her to know he said anything. I'll talk with the EMT guy, in fact, I'd better find him right now and tell him not to say anything except to the police. Be back later. Are you going to stick around here for awhile?"

"I'm not going anywhere until I hear how the surgery has gone. The doctor told Lorelie Jason's condition is critical. He has lost a great deal of blood. His blood pressure and other vital signs are significantly low. They are giving him blood and will operate soon as he is prepared for surgery by the anesthesiologist. Loreli was asked if her husband had any illnesses, diabetes or other conditions and what drugs does he take. He asked her specifically if Jason had taken anything this evening. Loreli said no to all questions.

"I better get back to Loreli in the waiting room. I don't want to take my eyes off of her," said Brooksie. Marino gave her a parting hug and told her he would see her later.

Time passed slowly in the waiting area and they were the only two in the room. Brooksie was becoming more uncomfortable alone with Loreli.

"Loreli would you like to go to the cafeteria and get something to eat and drink? We may have a long wait."

"Sure, that's a good idea. I'm glad I told you about Jason's depression. I thought he was going to leave the house right after me. He was talking about the last session. If I hadn't gone to the gym this wouldn't have happened. I will always blame myself." She wiped her eyes which didn't appear to need it and blew her nose.

Brooksie remained silent, kept her eyes focused on the her coffee cup, afraid of what fear and anger would show up on her face.

They found their way to the cafeteria and got coffee. They sat for a few minutes without conversing. Detectives Swain and Marino showed up at their table.

"Can we join you two ladies?" asked Swain.

The second their presence was registered by Loreli she began to sob again wiping away those invisible tears. Her eye makeup remained perfect. Marino sat next to Loreli. She grabbed his hand and held on for dear life.

"If I hadn't left for the gym he wouldn't be dying. I'll never be able to forgive myself."

The detective gently removed his hand from her death grip and took a cup of coffee offered by his partner. "Joe, this is Loreli. Loreli, this is my partner Detective Swain."

"Nice to meet you Detective Swain."

"Could I speak to you privately on another matter Detective Marino? It won't take long," asked Brooksie."

Loreli looked pleadingly at Marino then quickly moved her dry-eyed focus to Swain.

"We will be just fine, won't we Mrs. Woods?" responded Swain.

"Maybe you would be kind enough to get me a refill Detective Swain? asked Loreli.

"With pleasure ma'am."

Brooksie and Marino walked into the hallway, out of earshot.

"Blake, have you talked with the EMT that was in the back of the ambulance with Jason? He heard what I did from Jason."

"I told Sharp what you said and she will take care of the interview."

Brooksie continued, "When you and Swain showed up, Loreli started to sob, but not one tear was visible. I know everyone handles a crisis differently, but I swear she's not thinking about Jason except afraid he will survive. If he does make it what's to stop her from trying again?"

"You may be jumping to conclusions. Was Jason in any condition to know what he was saying?"

"Blake, he clearly said 'Loreli why why?' He didn't seem able to keep his eyes open for long. The attendant told me to keep talking to him to keep him awake if possible. This is so unbelievable.

"That woman scares me. At the same time I have the urge to tear her eyes out. She is acting. What a cold heart and twisted mind she must possess. I guess it is a miracle that Jason has lived long enough to make it to surgery."

"Detective Sharp said it looked like Jason had been lying on the floor for more than a few hours because the blood had coagulated around him. When the ambulance guys started to move him onto the gurney, he was curled up and his torso was pushed against the bundled up rug. That pressure from the rug and his position may be the reason he didn't bleed out immediately. As soon as he was moved, a large amount of blood came gushing out of the abdominal area. They were able to quickly stop the flow with hand held pressure. That kept him from losing any more blood.

Marino continued, "If Jason survives the surgery, an officer will be posted in the room and outside the door."

"Loreli was supposed to accompany Jason to our office on Tuesday," added Brooksie. "We were going to ask them both to tell their stories in front of each other. I think she had a suspicion of what we were planning. Jason showed up, but said his wife complained of feeling sick and would come next week. She decided to put her evil plan in action earlier than she had originally wanted.

"Thanks for coming tonight. I have to admit one of my first thoughts, as Lucinda, Tony and I were driving over to Jason's house was how upset you would be with me, again. Knowing that I knew I would not stop doing what I thought needed to be done. I'm so sorry Blake. I can't be the kind of person you want and deserve."

"I knew we would butt heads on certain things. I can't change and you shouldn't either. Right now the focus is on Mr. Woods. If he makes it or not, there is police work to be done," responded Marino in a subdued voice.

Brooksie gave Marino a hug which he returned. They both understood there had been a significant shift in their future relationship. Marino looked down at his hands. Brooksie's lips quivered. Both looked sad.

As they returned to the table in the cafeteria, Loreli stood and told them she had just been paged to the surgery waiting room.

All four headed to the surgical floor joined by Lucinda and Tony.

Brooksie introduced Lucinda and Tony as staff members of the clinic, while they continued to hurry to their destination

"Is the whole clinic staff coming?" belted out Loreli, sounding slightly annoyed.

"We didn't think you should be alone at this terrible waiting time," answered Lucinda. "Have you heard anything yet?"

"No. Doctor Williams spoke with me before taking Jason into surgery and said my husband's condition was very serious. He didn't know how long surgery would take. That was several hours ago.

"I do appreciate your willingness to wait it out with me, but it's really not necessary. It's late and you all have jobs to go to tomorrow. I'll be fine."

"We wouldn't think of leaving you alone. We all care for Jason and believe he would expect us to offer you support, and if the worse happens to offer comfort," responded Brooksie.

Loreli shrugged, turned abruptly and entered the waiting room, sat down and began to pick at her meticulously manicured nails.

Detectives Swain and Marino announced they would be hanging around until the doctor returned with news.

Brooksie had decided she would shadow Loreli every minute. She couldn't say anything to Lucinda or Tony, placing Loreli under suspicion. She trusted that Marino would take any and all precautionary steps to protect Jason if he survived surgery.

Letting her mind flow back to the hugs she and Marino shared a short time ago, sadness engulfed her. There was an unspoken good-bye that was felt and delivered by both when they tenderly hugged for the last time.

Marino was such a good man. She would miss him. *Eventually we would hurt each other. Better to end it now and work through my grief than later when we might have children. I could never leave him if we had children, that is so selfish and hurtful of the innocent. I have felt that childhood confusion and pain more than once. I never want to do that to a child of mine.*

Maybe I should take a short vacation. I could go see Abby in California. She's a good listener. Better stay away from Aunt Tilly.

She can spot my moods a mile away and decide what I need is another pet. I could wind up with a few goats and whatever else she has in abundance. No. Stay away from Aunt Tilly for a while.

Dr. Williams entered the room and put an end to Brooksie's thoughts.

"Mrs. Woods I have good news. Not great, but good. Jason has survived surgery and is in the intensive care unit. He is not completely out of the woods, yet. The next twenty-four to forty-eight hours will tell us much more about his recovery.

"It seems a possibility that after your husband was shot, the position he fell into, all curled up, slowed down the blood loss and that is what gave him this chance to survive."

Loreli's face blanched, she was visibly shaken.

The doctor nturally assumed it was the shock of the near death of her husband and the continued worry about his survival that had turned her so pale.

"I know all of this has been a frightening experience for you. Please sit down."

He poured water into a paper cup from the nearby dispenser and handed it to her.

"I'm okay. Thank you. When can I see him?"

"In a few hours. Someone will come here and take you to his room."

"Are you saying he could still die?"

"He has a good chance for survival Mrs. Woods. Your husband's age and physical condition are all in his favor. There is something I need to clear up. You said earlier that he does not take any medications other than aspirin. Is that correct?"

"Yes. Why?"

"The anesthesiologist had some questions, he will catch up to you sometime today and run them by you."

Loreli appeared to compose herself and addressing no one in particular said, "Maybe I should go home and get a few things. I plan to stay the night here."

"There is a recliner in the room with your husband which many find very comfortable and permit some sleep. It is totally up to you if you spend the night or not."

"I feel it is my place to be by his side until he is out of the woods. Thank you for all you have done."

Brooksie felt a chill go up her spine She looked over at Marino and he gave her a nod letting her know he understood her concern for the safety of Jason.

Loreli asked where the restrooms were located. She was given directions and she left the room. The minute she went out the door, Brooksie told Lucinda to go with Loreli and come back when she comes back. She'd explain later.

Lucinda did what she had been asked.

Marino motioned for Brooksie to meet him in the hallway. "A policeman will be in the room with Jason at all times and one will be at the door. If Loreli is the shooter, she will soon become suspicious and who knows what she will do. Hopefully, Jason wakes up and is lucid and will repeat what he told you. Detective Sharp and I are going to talk with the surgeon in a few minutes. Let him know what we are considering about the wife and see if he has anything to share. Also, it sounds important for me or Detective Sharp to speak with the anesthesiologist."

"I'll stick around for a little while. Lucinda, Tony and I are all beat and you've got everything covered. Marino, I believe Jason. I get a bad feeling around Loreli. She wants to get rid of him and if she gets the chance she will try again."

"Go home and get some rest. I'll call if anything changes."

CHAPTER THIRTY-THREE

"You can do anything in this world if you're
prepared to take the consequences
W. Somerset Maugham - *The Circle*

It was almost 1 a.m. when Brooksie dragged herself through her front door. There was a note on the island in the kitchen from her neighbors. She had called them hours before and asked them to feed her menagerie dinner as she wouldn't get home till very late.

The note read, "Glad you called and of course we fed, played and kissed them good-night. Hope all is okay. Let us know if we can do anything else." Signed Randy.

Brooksie pulled off her clothes and let them stay where they fell. Plopped herself into bed and one minute later was softly snoring.

The phone rang and Brooksie jumped several inches into the air, sat straight up bleary eyed before she realized she was hearing the phone.

"Hello," she responded; through a raspy and dry throat.

"Hon, it's me Marino. Sorry to wake you."

"What time is it? What's going on? Is Jason okay?"

"Whoa, hon. One question at a time. First off it's 6 a.m. Jason woke up, saw Loreli in the chair next to his bed and started yelling 'get out, get out'. He tried to get out of the bed, but was restrained by the nurse and the officer. The officer suggested to Loreli she might step outside the door until her husband could calm down. She did what was suggested.

"The surgeon just happened to come early to make rounds and he told Loreli outside in the hall, Jason was responding very well and should fully recover. He would probably remain hospitalized for several more days."

Loreli told the doctor she didn't understand why Jason had yelled at her to get out. Dr. Williams did a great job of covering up the fact that she was the main suspect at this hour. He suggested she might want to go home, freshen up and even sleep for a while then return to the hospital and Jason would probably be more like himself.

"We arrested her in the parking lot. Didn't want to have to do it in the hospital and cause a scene or put anyone in danger. As it turned out, she did throw a temper fit, yelling, crying and just as quickly got hold of herself and asked Detective Sharp what the charge was.

"She was told it was attempted homicide. Her answer, 'You are making a terrible mistake. I have been to the police department and told Detective Marino all about my concerns and fears regarding Jason. He has problems and he blames me. I've even shared my concerns with Ms. Everett of the clinic. My husband shot himself. He had been threatening to for a long time. Make him tell you the truth. Surely, you're not going to put those handcuffs on me?'

The female officer cuffed Loreli and helped her into the back seat of the patrol car. Loreli quickly composed herself and politely asked to have her sweater placed over her shoulders complaining of being cold. That was done and she was driven to the precinct.

She's truly a work of art. A beautifully wrapped package with garbage inside.

"After she was booked, she asked to call her lawyer, Mr. Podd, a well-known, mucho expensive, top notch criminal attorney. He has handled and freed some serious dudes in the past. I think he will have his hands full this time.

"This info is not for publication Brooksie. Jason was shot on the left side, just missing his heart. The doc said since Jason is right handed it would have been impossible for him to shoot himself in the place where the bullet entered. The angle and the trajectory will prove he couldn't have pulled the trigger himself. By this afternoon the doc assured Sharp and myself that Jason will be able to give a clear and precise description of what took place yesterday and at what time.

"Luckily for Jason, his wife was in a big hurry to get to the gym so she didn't check him out close enough to see he was still barely breathing. She also mistakenly placed the gun near the wrong hand. She was in such a hurry that she forgot he was right handed. Guess she never stood over his shoulder while he wrote checks.

"I have to admit hon, your gut feelings and the clinic squad you put together probably also saved his bacon. If you hadn't discovered his predicament when you did, he might not have had a ghost of a chance. I can see it now, the banner hanging over your office building. It could read, The Grief Clinic Detective Agency."

"Maybe more like The Detectives Support Squad," joked Brooksie. Marino, can I now tell Lucinda and Tony that Jason is recovering so far and Loreli has been arrested for attempted murder of her husband?"

"Sure. Just keep Jason's statement to yourself for now and any other details you are aware of."

"I would also like to tell the divorce group he has been part of, he was wounded and is now recovering. They have formed friendships and he is going to need some emotional support in the near future. Perhaps they would be permitted to visit him in the hospital with the doctor's okay.

"Thanks again, Blake. You are the best."

CHAPTER THIRTY-FOUR

**Happiness Makes Up in Height
for What It Lacks in Length**
Robert Frost - (poem title)

Four weeks later as preplanned, the divorce group, including the recovering Jason, meet at the Book End Bookstore.

Kent and Marlene had arranged and paid for the catering. Minestrone soup, shredded lettuce with black olives and parmesan cheese salad, and the main course was crab-stuffed raviolis.

The room was decked out with two beautiful flower arrangements, each one sitting on the large round tables set up for twelve at each table.

Guests started arriving one right after the other. It seemed no one wanted to be late for this show-and-tell day. A celebration of moving forward. Tony, Lucinda and Tony's daughter Katrina were the first to arrive. Followed immediately by Brooksie and Detective Marino. Brooksie hugged Marlene and complimented her for how festive the room looked and on the gorgeous flower arrangements.

"Marlene, you have added so much to this special get-together. Your generosity is a well- known fact, but you are more than that. You have a giving soul. Thank you so much. I appreciate how very special you have made this reunion."

"My pleasure," responded Marlene. "I really mean that. I love to plan events and watch people enjoy themselves. So you see, I'm being selfish."

"The world needs more selfish people like you," added the detective.

Shannon, Melika, Ruth and Cecelia all walked in arm and arm. Not easy going through a doorway. They had to walk sideways bantering in a joking way.

It took several minutes for the "Wows" and "Oh My Gods" and other words of amazement from those already in the room.

"You guys look fantastic!" from the chorus of three.

Ruth had a short-style hair cut which had been ever so lightly highlighted. She had on a long, teal colored skirt with a white silk blouse and a matching teal jacket. She looked elegant and almost unrecognizable. A light touch of rouge and lipstick completed her new look.

Lucinda and Brooksie didn't even try to wipe away their happy tears for Ruth's appearance. Tony whistled at the ladies and danced Ruth around the room. The smile on Ruth's face was pure joy.

Shannon appeared somewhat thinner and was attired in a flattering sea-blue pant suit. Her new haircut emphasized her high cheekbones and showed off her straight white teeth. She gave the impression of possessing an inborn strength by the way she held her head high and shoulders back. One learned from life experiences and the courage from facing up to the challenges. Her son by her side, was beaming as he escorted her to a table. The two formed a mutual admiration society.

Melika was wearing a robin-egg-colored knee-length dress. The color matched her beautiful eyes.

Her children looked like little clones. The girl's dresses matched their mothers as did the boy's shirt.

Cecelia appeared liked a proud mother hen of her three chicks. Some highlights had been added to her graying dark brown hair. The hairstylist had done a fine job of softening her features with more of a casual style haircut. A quick wash, blow dry and ready-for-the-day kind of style.

Jason timidly stood in the doorway. HIs guest gently pushed him forward into the room. When the others saw him, some began to sniffle and all started clapping.

Jason looked rather worse for wear. Somewhat thinner which was especially noticeable in his face. He introduced his neighbor lady and told those present, "This dear lady, my neighbor and friend for many years, Mrs. Lance, warned me about Loreli even before we were married. I'm sorry I brought such tragedy to the wonderful people of the clinic. I deeply regret Melissa's death.

"I also invited Shaun here today because he helped to bring Loreli to justice.

Handshakes, hugs, compliments and other warm greetings and words of praise and affection went on until Brooksie suggested everyone should find a chair and sit down.

Gage was the last one to enter, followed by a very attractive woman. When Gage noticed Jason, he stretched out his arms, gesturing for permission to hug.

"I won't break, Gage," said Jason through a giant smile. The two men embraced, Gage did so carefully.

"Are you one hundred percent now or what?" asked Gage.

"My wound is healing, but my spirit and self-confidence has a way to go."

"We are here for you buddy. I want to introduce you all to my better half. This is Gina and I want to share with all of you she has given me a second chance to get it right."

Gina blushed. The redness started at her neckline and moved quickly up and engulfed her entire face.

"Gage, we are both being given a second chance. We both had lessons to learn. I'm really pleased to meet all of you. Gage has told me wonderful things about each one of you including the brilliant staff.

"Brilliant? and I thought we were simply incredibly lucky. Joking aside, we sincerely appreciate your kind words," said Brooksie showing off a ear-to-ear grin.

Tony sat next to Ruth. Ruth's daughter sat next to one of Melika's young daughters. Both started whispering to each other and soon the giggles followed.

During the next two hours a delicious meal was consumed and a kind of progress report was shared by all of the previous members of the group.

Jason eventually told the group the details of his wife's attempt on his life and the murder of Melissa.

"I had often shared with Melissa several pictures of Loreli many Thursday evenings before group time. It embarrasses me to admit just how shallow and insensitive I was. I was showing off my trophy wife; makes me sick to my stomach just to say the truth about myself. Nevertheless, Melissa was always so kind and would say nice things about Loreli.

"I recently learned Melissa often went dancing and dining at The Barn with her boyfriend Shaun." Jason patted Shaun on the shoulder. He as seated next to him.

The Thursday night before the Thursday when she tried to do me in, Loreli also went to The Barn with some guy from the gym where she was a member.

Apparently, Melissa recognized her from the pictures I'd been showing her. Both women wound up in the rest room at the same time and Melissa must have said to Loreli that she recognized her from the pictures I had shown her.

"I'm assuming that my evil and hateful wife panicked when she realized Melissa would probably tell me about seeing her with some guy at The Barn dancing and whatever else she saw them doing.

Lorelli wasn't about to let her plans of getting rid of me and collecting the inheritance go up in smoke. She planned to make my death look like a suicide. She had been working on convincing others I was suicidal and if that didn't work, she would have switched to defense. She told others I was abusing her and became so violent she feared for her life. That would then give her the opportunity to claim she shot me trying to defend herself. How could I have been so blind?"

Mrs. Lance patted his hand and wiped her eyes. "You are a good man. None of this is your fault except maybe for not looking below the flawless face."

"I thank you all for your kindness and much needed support during this nightmare."

The meal was over and Marlene tapped her glass and asked for everyone's attention. "Our dessert will be served by the pie-baking lady herself. Ruth please come to the front and tell us what our choices are."

Ruth pushed back her chair and proud as a peacock announced she offered four kinds of pies: apple, peach, banana cream and her favorite, a chocolate mint cream pie.

"There's plenty for all. I make extra large pies 'cause I'm used to baking for a church crowd."

"I would like to say this has been a memorable, life affirming afternoon for me," announced Brooksie. "It demonstrated what a small group can accomplish, a group made up of people with similar problems who are willing to listen and share secrets, heartaches, insights and compassion for one another.

"The makeovers that Cecelia made possible was icing on the cake. You all worked hard at your individual makeovers on the inside. Be proud of yourselves and of each other. I surely am.

"I miss Melissa and will not forget her. I will also remember each one of you for the lessons I've learned from your willingness to make changes and to leave the tunnel vision and old habits in the past.

"I don't like good-byes, so I'm not going to say those words. I choose to say, see you."

CHAPTER THIRTY-FIVE

**'Tis better to have loved and lost
Than never to have loved at all.**
Alfred, Lord Tennyson - In Memoriam

Detective Marino drove Brooksie to her home after leaving the Book Ends Bookstore, which gave them some visiting time.

"That was the most meaningful and emotional reunion I've had the pleasure of attending. Do you think there is any possibility Loreli will get away with murder and the failed attempt with Jason?"

"Evidence is piling up against her, but murderers have been known to get off on a technicality. She has a hell of a sharp attorney. He has the reputation of beating the system and getting the perpetrator off the hook.

"Loreli is one piece of work. She may have also done in her last husband. It seems the sister of the deceased husband, living in England has been in touch with our department. Loreli was married to some rich old in England. His death was suspicious, so Loreli left under a cloud of innocence. Her greedy nature may be the nail in the coffin. When Jason's house was gone through for the second time, a locket containing Melissa's picture was found. It was stuffed in the toe of a shoe placed in a shoe box. Loreli's fingerprints were on it. The theory is Loreli may be the kind of killer who likes to keep some trophy or remembrance. The evidence is piling up against her and we do have an eye witness, Jason himself. I don't see any way for her to get out of this. She hasn't been able to come up with the bail. Apparently, she's run out of suckers. Even one of her lover boys from the gym is pointing the finger at her."

"I just had a terrible thought," exclaimed Brooksie.

"What if Loreli ended up in the Women's prison with Sharon. My colleagues and I could even have her in one of our workshops. I'm not that nice of a person to want to help that evil bitch."

"You know how I feel about your plans to work at the prison. I'm not going to change my mind."

"I know, Blake. I see your side and appreciate your safety concerns for everyone involved. If Sharon's programs are accepted and Lucinda, Rachael and I are accepted, I will enthusiastically participate when the warden gives the go ahead."

Marino pulled into Brooksie's driveway and parked. He turned off the engine and said, "How do you see this going down between us hon?"

Brooksie began to tear up and took hold of his hands.

"You are such a fine man. I love so much about you and how you make me feel safe and secure, desirable and loved. Child adoption and my work are huge obstacles. I don't believe either of us should have to change, you said the same thing, about a month ago. If I gave in and had our kids, gave up my work, it wouldn't be long before resentments raised their ugly heads. If you were to concede, the results would be the same. You have expectations of a wife and I'm not willing to live up to them. One day we might both be miserable.

"Giving birth is not a burning desire for me. I have seen too many children who need caring homes, kids who are neglected, abandoned and abused, parents unfit to raise even a gerbil and can cause life-long damage to their offspring. I don't have the need to raise my own flesh and blood kids.

"You and foster kids are not an option. You see them as permanently damaged and I see them as temporarily wounded. I do believe you will make a great father and husband. I don't know if I will do as well, as a wife and mother."

"I wish I could change my feelings about raising another man's child, but I can't. Maybe it's my ego talking. My dad felt the same way and I guess he made a permanent impression on me.

"So are we really going to go our separate ways? You sure you want that?"

"My heart doesn't want to let us end, but to stay together requires changes that neither of us wants to make. Later we would be sorry, sad and miserable. If we disagreed on minor issues we could work those out, both giving a little. I think our differences are major and they were tattooed on our hearts, probably sometime during our childhood. Tattoos are usually permanent and if removed leave a mark."

They clung to each other. Marino blew his nose and ran his sleeve over his eyes. Brooksie sobbed softly, moved away and exited the car. She watched his car as he slowly drove away.

CHAPTER THIRTY-SIX

To love is a privilege,
To be loved is an honor.

Six months later.......

Luke Jones, the landscaper, transformed Brooksie's yards months earlier. He continued to be her gardener, coming every two weeks to cut lawn, prune and whatever else needed looking after. There were interesting stone pathways leading through flower gardens graced by two arbors, both covered with vines. One, a grape ivy vine which had quickly begun to cover the arbor and was reaching for the attached fence.

All the dogs and several cats made daily trips through the backyard. Luke had planned for several cat hideaways and trees calling out to be climbed.

The dogs could chase each other at full speed through the back yard and when the gate was opened they could continue their cavorting into the front yard. They would romp and wrestle on the grassy areas. Samson, the cat who thought he was a dog, would try to join in, but soon discovered the play was too rough for him.

Brooksie had finally agreed to a tennis date with Luke and his now-adopted son Drake.

The third time on the court, Drake was given his own small racket. He tried hard to hit the ball. On a few occasions the ball actually went over the net much to Drake's excitement and Luke's surprise.

After some time on the court and rallying back and forth, Brooksie and Luke had worked up a sweat.

"Let's call it a day," panted Luke. "Would you go to dinner with me tonight? I'd like to take you to my favorite place. It's called Luigis's, a family run restaurant. The food is spectacular. Do you like Italian?"

"I love food period. Especially Italian and Mexican. I would like to go to dinner with you. What time and is it casual?" Brooksie, I'm not a suit and tie kind of guy. New Levis are as close as I get to dressing up. I'll pick you up at six. I've got a great baby sitter for Drake. He loves her 'cause she plays hide and seek with him. Mrs. Walsh is a widow and lives near me. One night when I returned home Drake and Mrs. Walsh were dressed up as pirates. Her own children are grown and live in other states. I think she gets lonely, probably missing family. Drake is like a grandchild for her. I'm so lucky to have her.

"My own folks help out when they can, but they both have busy lives. They love Drake and are great grandparents, but Mrs. Walsh will get down and dirty, literally, with Drake."

"You are very fortunate to have such a caring sitter," remarked Brooksie.

"I also want to know if you would like to come to the court house when Drake's adoption becomes official."

"Wow, what an honor. Yes, I would love to be there. I was adopted when I was a baby, so I have no memories of any kind of ceremonies. I may get teary-eyed and embarrass you."

"No problem. I'll be too busy embarrassing myself making weird sounds trying to stop myself from sobbing."

Luke reminded Brooksie he would pick her up at six. They left the tennis courts, got into their cars and drove off.

Brooksie, at home, played and fed her pet companions. She took a shower and dressed in a white peasant blouse, a long multicolored skirt and sandals. *It feels strange going on a actual date, almost like I'm cheating on Marino. I wish it wasn't an Italian place. That brings back even more memories That's crazy. It's been over six months since we broke up. I'm just going to dinner. Don't be so ridiculous."*

Luke drove up in a Suburban. Brooksie waved, closed the front door and asked, "Where is the famous work truck?"

"This is my go-to-town transportation and now that I'm going to be an official dad I wanted something more family friendly. It's not brand new, but new to me. Only has twenty-thousand miles on it and was a fair price. Do you like it?'

"Yes I really like the color. It's kind of a pewter. Lots of room inside. Looks like it can carry six adults or more children plus pets."

"That's the idea. Family Services contacted me with information about fostering more kids. You've mentioned your interest in the foster program. The department is putting on an information event in a few weeks. I can give you the time and how to sign up if you like?"

"Yes, give me that info and I'll go if I can. Actually I'm more interested in adoption. I'm not sure I could take a child for a short time and then have to give them up. This is why I have so many pets. Aunt Tilly knows my weaknesses. Once I have a pet in my possession for a few days I'm hopelessly attached. I think it would be the same if I was caring for a child.

"Didn't you fall in love with Drake soon after you began fostering him?"

"Absolutely, but I did find out after he moved in with me it was very unlikely his parents or relatives would ever take him. You have some say in what child you foster. You can always say no. The social workers are great and will have some idea as to the adoptability of the foster child."

"I'll give the department a call and talk with someone. It does scare me to think about being responsible for a child. Maybe I won't be any good at it."

"I'm not trying to talk you in to anything. Check out the information and see for yourself how you feel. No hurry, no commitment, only a time to gather information."

Their conversation was politely interrupted by Maria, who brought them their salads. Maria owned and operated the restaurant with her husband Luigi. They owned the business for twenty years. Maria had quite a reputation as a wise woman and she was known for never holding back her advice.

"Who is this lovely lady, Luke? Finally you bring in someone for me to look over. Introduce us."

"This is Brooksie, Mama Sorento."

"Nice to meet you, Mrs. Sorento."

"You must call me Maria or Mama Sorento." "Nice to meet you Maria," responded Brooksie.

"Mama Sorento is like a mother to all who come through her doors. She is not only a fantastic chef, but gives free advice with her meals," added Luke.

"Have you known Luke long?" asked Maria.

"Yes, for about six months. I've played tennis with him and his son several times and he landscaped my yard and did a fine job of it."

"So this is the first date, huh? I get a very good feeling about you two. You are wearing new Levis tonight, Luke. A good sign for your future."

Maria winked at Luke and hurried off to the kitchen.

"What a delightful character, so warm and friendly. I can see why the customers call her Mama. Thanks for bringing me here."

They took plenty of time eating and conversing. After dessert they said their good-byes to 'Mama' and promised to return soon.

At Brooksie's door, she thanked Luke profusely for a delightful time. He turned to go down the steps, hesitated, walked back up, pulled her towards him and kissed her willing mouth. The kiss started out tenderly, but quickly became more intense. When they separated and their breathing slowed to normal Luke again walked down the steps and continued on to his car. With a big grin on his face he drove off.

Brooksie's hands shook while she turned the key into the lock and entered to the excited barks and shows of affection from a number of the pets. Several cats took their own time to show pleasure for her return.

"Wish I could be more cat-like. Stand-offish, reserved, but shit, I'm like my dogs, tail wagging like a mad drummer, jumping up and down with tongue hanging out. Damn I was ready to tear my clothes off and his in one quick movement. I'll never get to sleep tonight."

CHAPTER THIRTY-SEVEN

For, you see, each day I love you more.
Today more than yesterday and
less than tomorrow.
Rosemonde Gerard - *L'eternelle chanson*

Not long after the clinic's reunion, Lucinda and Tony are finished up another divorce group. They would often go for coffee and dessert at the Table Talk Cafe after the evening group disbanded.

Tony and Lucinda's relationship had grown into a beautiful love affair. Tony's daughter had become very fond of Lucinda and truly bonded with her. She missed having a mother figure in her life, like so many of her friends had. She loved her dad, but she was beginning to feel more in step with her peers since her dad brought Lucinda into their life. Lucinda and Katrina did girl things together. They liked shopping for clothes and once even had a manicure.

Now Tony had two unpaid editors and readers for his ever growing book writing, Lucinda and Katrina. The maternal grandparents were happy for Tony and their granddaughter to have Lucinda gradually become part of the family.

Lucinda was blossoming under the loving and accepting eyes of Tony.

Tony planned a secret birthday party for Lucinda with Brooksie, Anita and Rachael as co-conspirators. He reserved the Table Talk Cafe's back room for the surprise to be held on Friday night.

Rachael and Anita took on the job of decorating and Brooksie did the food ordering. The cafe was to do the catering. The menu for the party read; Italian wedding soup, spinach salad with cranberries and walnuts, homemade sourdough bread, and the main dish, a stuffed pork roast. The dessert was to be furnished by Tony.

That evening, Tony picked up Lucinda and told her he needed to make a quick stop at the Table Talk Cafe before heading for the Fish House for their dinner date. He had asked her to dress up slightly more than usual. "This is a special birthday and I want you to remember it always," said Tony.

While they drove to the cafe, multiple complements were passed back and forth as to how handsome or beautiful the other looked.

Lucinda was wearing a long dress in a sea-foam color, form-fitting with spaghetti straps and the skirt flowed loosely from the waist. She was wearing her hair down touching her shoulders, and earrings matching the color of her dress completed the look.

They pulled into the parking lot of the cafe. Few cars in the lot. "I'll be right back Lucy, only take a minute."

He quickly walked to the back room and saw all was ready and the guests standing around whispering to each other. "I'll be back in a second with Lucy."

Tony raced back to his car, breathless his heart rate doubled and asked Lucinda if she would mind coming in for a minute because his business was taking a little longer than he planned.

Lucinda followed him in and together they walked to the back. He opened the door and everyone yelled, "Happy birthday Lucy."

She nearly tripped over her long skirt trying to jump back. Both hands flew to cover her wide open mouth. "Wh..... My God I can't believe this. Whose ideas was this? Tony did you do this?"

"Your friends all pitched in after I asked them about a surprise for you. They simply caught the fever and had a great time planning and preparing."

Lucinda tried unsuccessfully to catch the wet drops coming from her eyes with her hands. Brooksie and Anita both wiped the moisture moving down their cheeks. Lucinda then joyfully and with hugs, greeted everyone present. "I can't believe so many kept this a secret. Even you Katrina, my little sweet pea. I must remember what a good secret keeper you are."

Tony's daughter beamed and skipped off with Luke's son Drake. The two kids had already made up a game giving their imaginations free range, as only children can do with such abandonment.

Brad, Anita's brother, proudly introduced his date Lin, a petite Japanese girl. "Anita and Lin attend the same university. My sister introduced me to Lin, we dated briefly and that's all she wrote. We are engaged. Guess our romance took off like wild fire."

Brooksie made the rounds introducing Luke. Lucinda and Tony had met him a few months back.

Tony gently steered Lucinda over to meet Mr. & Mrs. Spinoza. "These are my dear in-laws Lucy."

"It is such a pleasure to meet you. Tony has spoken of you often and with such love and appreciation for your constant support and understanding. I'm so sorry about the loss of your daughter."

"Thank you for your kind words. Tony is the best father any child could ever have. He has told us about you and what wonderful work you do at the clinic. Our dear granddaughter is also taken by you. She goes on and on talking about all the fun the three of you have," said Mrs. Spinoza.

Mr. Spinoza added, "We are so happy you are in their lives and now maybe we can also join in the fun."

"You two would be a wonderful addition. We must plan some activity for all of us very soon," said Lucinda.

The room was abuzz with happy sounds, lots of laughter and teasing. Eventually the meal was served and quickly finished, dishes cleared away and Rachael and Brooksie appeared pushing in the food cart that was bearing a large cake.

Tony took Lucinda by the hand and led her to the cake. The rest gathered around them. Tony asked her to close her eyes which she did. When she was standing in front of the cart, she could hear several gasps and a few "wows."

"Open your eyes Lucy." She did, blinked a few times and looked down. There was a white sheet cake with the words, 'Will you marry me, please', written in bright colors.

Lucinda covered her face with both hands and tears trickled down her cheeks through her spread fingers. She put her arms around Tony's neck between sobs "Oh. yes, yes eagerly and happily. I never imagined loving someone and being loved back could feel like this, indescribable."

Tony handed her a small box which she tried to open, her hands were too shaky and Tony opened the box for her. Inside was a beautiful yellow diamond engagement ring.

"Oh's and ahs", congratulations and other joyful sounds filled the room. Many happy tears were being shed, nose blowing, laughter, and abundance of hugs made it around this group bonded by adversity.

Tony placed the ring on her finger, she kissed him and her new daughter to be. "I feel so blessed to have you as my very own daughter and so grateful you are willing to share your dad with me. I can't take your mother's place, but I hope you will make room for me."

"What do I call you now?"

"You've been calling me Lucy so whatever you're comfortable with is okay by me."

"How about mama Lucy? I like that.

"Lucinda started to cry in earnest this time and simply wrapped her arms around her new offspring.

Slowly, the happy guests started leaving. Mrs. Long, Katrina's sitter and part time housekeeper walked out with Katrina followed closely by most of the others.

The last to leave were Brooksie, Luke, Lucinda, and Tony.

"There is a gift from Rachael and Anita in Luke's car. We didn't want you to open it before Tony sprung his proposal because of the intimacy of the gift, might have proven embarrassing to a few."

The four sat awhile soaking in the plethora of feelings, all loving and listened to Tony and Lucinda discuss wedding and honeymoon plans.

CHAPTER THIRTY-EIGHT

A hard beginning maketh a good ending.
John Heywood - Proverbs

Approximately one year after the murder of Melissa and attempted killing of Jason, Melissa's boyfriend, Shaun, showed up at the Grief Clinic office. He asked the secretary if he could see Brooksie Everett.

Miss Jackson, the secretary, knocked on Brooksie's door.

"Come in, Shirley."

"A young man calling himself Shaun is asking to see you."

"Oh, fantastic. I'll meet him myself."

Brooksie went to the door and called, "Shaun, please come in. Good to see you."

"Thanks Miss Everett."

"Please call me Brooksie."

"Okay Brooksie. I just left the court house and Loreli Woods has been found guilty on all counts of murder and attempted murder. The prosecutor told me the sentencing will come later. He believes she will get life. I've never known anyone so evil. She never changed her expressions during the months of trial. I swear she tried to seduce every male in the room, focusing on the prosecutor and judge. Her own attorney was a woman so she didn't bother to put her moves on a female. Although if she thought it would help I think she'd switch in a second.

"Melissa didn't need or deserve to die. I still miss her a lot. I'm thinking of moving out of the area for a while, too many memories and too many ghosts.

"By the way, the prosecutor thinks she will be sent to that prison where you and the other social workers are doing some kind of work. I seem to remember you mentioned Lancers Women's Prison. Loreli will soon to be calling that place home."

"Yes, that's the prison where we are offering workshops. It would be disconcerting if she wound up in one of our workshops, but I don't think they let people doing time for murder attend our programs.

"I understand you wanting to get a fresh start. I wish you much happiness, new adventures and new relationships. You are a caring, decent man. Grief is about turning a page when you feel ready to. Are you going to stick around to hear the sentence for Mrs. Woods before you leave town?"

"No. That could take too long. I'm not trying to rush away, just making a plan. Melissa often talked about Hawaii. She said the weather was sunny and warm year round, different from here. She told me the life is laid back. No one in a hurry. That would suit me fine. I'm thinking about starting out in Maui because she had read up on it and we were planning to vacation there one day. I haven't quite made up my mind which island. Do you want me to let you know where I land?"

"I would appreciate that, Shaun. A postcard would be nice. The other social workers are also interested in how you are making out. Thanks for coming by. Aloha, my friend."

Two weeks later Shaun called the clinic leaving a message for Brooksie. The message read, 'she will be going to Lancers Women's prison for a short time then transferred somewhere else. She got thirty-five years to life. Good-bye to you and the wonderful staff. I'm leaving for Maui in five days. I'll send a postcard soon as I get settled. Shaun.'

"Oh shit," responded Brooksie louder than she had meant to..

"What's wrong Brooksie? I heard you all the way down the hall.?" said Lucinda.

"Sorry, Shaun left me a message that said Loreli will be housed at Lancers for a short time and then transferred. Life sure takes strange turns at times. Five of us from the clinic and Loreli in the same place. Should prove interesting."

Lancers Women's Prison

Dr. Primm's workshops had been going on for many months prior to the arrival of the new inmate, Loreli Woods.

Lucinda, Rachael, Anita and Brooksie had all received clearance to teach the workshops. Two workshops with different agendas were offered every two weeks. That means that Lucinda and Rachael worked one half day a month at the prison and Brooksie and Anita worked the other two workshops once a month. This lessened the hardship for the four of them. They only had to make the trip to and from the prison once a month. They committed themselves to a one-year contract.

Dr. Primm and two of the social workers ran the two-hour workshops. Sharon attended every workshop.

The news of Loreli's pending arrival and short stay at the Lancer's Prison, gave the five much to talk about. Their thoughts turned to Melissa and the near death of Jason. They spoke frequently to one another, bonded by their own anxieties and the seesaw of up and down feelings.

Brooksie thought to herself, *This may prove to be interesting. Loreli being housed in such close proximity to us. I doubt she'll be there very long. I miss Marino sometimes, but mostly I'm glad we have gone our separate ways. I am myself with Luke. He is so easy to be with. Aunt Tilly finally got her wish and matched me up. She is definitely the number one matchmaker and not only for pets.*

Printed in the United States
By Bookmasters